LINGERING INNOCENCE

Lingering Innocence

Maya Scott

PALMETTO

PUBLISHING

Charleston, SC

www.PalmettoPublishing.com

Hardcover ISBN: 979-8-8229-4084-0
Paperback ISBN: 979-8-8229-3958-5

For my family, I treasure all of you. I feel beyond blessed to know and love each and every one of you.

This book is dedicated to my grandpa, James L. Bethea, Sr. He passed away before getting to see my book published. He was my best friend. I miss you, Grandpa.

If you or someone you love is a victim of sexual assault, I hear you, I see you, and most importantly, I believe you.

Content Warning

Lingering Innocence contains triggering and graphic material, including sexual assault and domestic violence. If you or someone you know needs support, resources are listed at the back of the book.

Chapter One

Dylan Spencer
Monday, October 31st, 12:00 p.m.

The musical arts hallway is filled with vibrant sounds as the orchestra plays. You can hear the instrumental tune of "Rather Be" playing all the way throughout the hallway. Brooklyn loves to play the violin. She's so good at it, but, then again, she's good at everything. Brooklyn's a biology major though. That girl loves a good book and stays in the science lab doing research. I always wondered how someone could love science as much as she does. Growing up, I hated science. I was never good at it. I mean, who needs or cares to know every single element on the periodic table? Beats me. As the orchestra slowly finishes their piece, I stick my head in the class. There she is, Brooklyn Reed. Her head is filled with beautiful curls in the shade of auburn brown. Her eyes are just as brown as her hair. Her eyes light up as they meet mine. She packs up her violin, puts it in her cabinet, and runs over to me. I see her every day, and every day she's just as excited to see me. It makes my heart race and makes me love her even more.

"Hey, Dyl," she said, hugging me.

I can't help but smile.

"Do you want to walk with me to the lab?" she asked.

"I'd want nothing more," I said with a smile. Morrid University is the most prestigious university in New York City. Not only are the academics impeccable here, but the arts and sports are just as impressive. The musical hallway leads us across the courtyard to the science building. I come to this building every day with her. I have a class all the way across the campus, giving me less than ten minutes to get there, but I don't mind. We get to "Advanced Neuroscience Lab 505." The name sounds so confusing, I give Brooklyn a kiss on the cheek and head back across the courtyard.

By the snack cart, I see Reese flirting with a guy. Nothing new. I can never keep up with his love triangles. Reese is my best friend. He has been since freshman year of high school, and he's never missed one of my games or wasn't there for me when I needed him.

Reese looks right at me, almost feeling caught. The look on his face was priceless because he's supposed to be in a relationship, but that doesn't stop him from flirting. He leaves the guy and walks right up to me.

"Don't say it," he said with an attitude.

I roll my eyes and walk with him to the dining hall. I should be heading to global studies right now, but God, I really want a cheeseburger. Reese hates any type of meaty food. He thinks it's filled with carbs and will make him "fat." If anything, that guy needs a bit more meat on his bones. Walking into the dining hall, you can just smell the food permeating the air. I walk directly to the cheeseburger line, and my mouth waters seeing everyone else enjoying their burger. I'm next in line, and Reese fakes a gag. I can't help but laugh. That guy is so dramatic that he needs his own television series.

"Are you sure you don't want a burger? Maybe even fries?" I said with a laugh.

"You couldn't pay me to eat this nasty, disgusting, and processed food." Reese said with disgust. I laugh and pick up a tray with a cheeseburger, fries, and water. Reese and I walk to our spot. We've sat at the same place every year in college. We're juniors now, which makes us feel so old at times. Watching the freshman squirm and get overwhelmed with the chaos in the dining hall.

"Dyl, I got to go. Nick wants to meet before his workout," Reese said with a bit of a grin. Reese gets so excited about Nick but can't seem to get out of his old habits. He gets up and walks out with his hands on his hips.

Like I said, this guy was a character. I unlock my phone to see a text from Brooke. "Hey, thinking about you. Midterms are next week for bio. Kind of want to die. LOL."

I smile. "You can always let me help you study." I texted along with a winky face emoji.

"Never going to happen, Goldilocks," she responded. She's been calling me Goldilocks since we first started dating. She says my hair makes it all make sense. I'm a natural blonde, and my curls are pretty nice, not as nice as hers, but close.

I finish my food and head to the trash can. Toss it in there and walk out. "Ding, Ding," my phone alerts me to let me know I got a new message. It's an emoji, the eyes. "Must be the wrong number," I said under my breath. I've been getting a lot of these messages for some reason. I just figured some freshman girls got my number and were messing around, which wasn't such a drastic thought. Girls throw themselves at me like it's nothing. I couldn't care less. If anything, that attention kind of makes me uncomfortable. Almost like they know I'm in a relationship, but they just don't care. Brooklyn says some girls are like that. They don't respect boundaries and have their own motives regardless of consequences. I delete the message and walk to global studies. I'm thirty minutes late, so when I get there, Professor Gwen rolls her eyes and sips her coffee. It's weird to drink coffee in the afternoon. It seems like the only time for it is breakfast. I take my seat, pull out my computer, and begin taking notes.

My phone dings again. My heart races a bit, thinking it's Brooklyn. But it's not. It's another random number. I open the message, and it's a Dropbox link. I click it out of curiosity, and it's filled with photos of me, but I'm not aware the pictures are being taken. "What the hell?" I said under my breath.

"Don't you get it? I'm always watching," said the message at the bottom of the screen. Like I said, this kind of stuff wasn't uncommon, but, not gonna lie, this freaked me out a bit.

Class feels like it's an eternity long. But hearing her say we can go makes my day. I was thinking about the message the whole class period. It was weird, very weird. I pack my stuff up and walk toward the door.

"Dylan Spencer," said Professor Gwen. "Why are you late today?" she said, crossing her arms.

"I stopped to eat," I answered.

"Dylan, your grades are amazing, and you work hard but don't abuse your freedom. I know your family is important here, but that doesn't mean special treatment." she said.

Not gonna lie, it felt like a slap in the face. I sigh and nod my head. I walked out, but I still felt really upset. Everything I have, I worked for. I did this, not my family. I shake off the thought of my family because I just didn't want to think about it anymore. I head back across the courtyard to the science building. Brooklyn's outside the classroom, talking to Mariah. Mariah's cool. She's as opinionated as ever and not afraid to let you know she doesn't like you.

"Hey, Blondie, aren't you going to be Peter Pan for Halloween?" Mariah said.

I had almost forgotten that today was Halloween. "Oh, Mariah, is this you saying you don't hate me anymore?" I teased.

"Not even close; you still suck," she said.

Brooklyn laughs.

Mariah's not happy with me at the moment. I tried to set her up with someone on the team for a double date with me and Brooke. Needless to say, it did not go well at all. But then again, Mariah's not a very friendly person, but she loves hard. On the other hand, Brooklyn's sort of the opposite. She's nice and sensitive, and she was a bit nervous to open her heart to me at first. But opposites attract in friendships, I guess.

"What are everyone's plans for tonight?" Mariah says.

"Not sure. Reese wanted to go to a party, but knowing him, it probably won't be my type of crowd," I said.

"I wanted to catch up on some research tonight," said Brooklyn.

"You guys utterly bore me. I'm out." Mariah said as she walked away. She and Reese really know how to make an exit.

As I'm walking back to the apartments on campus, I get an attachment message. I click on it, and it's a video of me walking. I look around, and I see no one. God, what is wrong with people? I walk into the lobby and get on the elevator. When your grandfather is the president of the university, you get cool stuff. The suite Reese and I live in is so nice. We're on the third floor and have a pretty nice place. I hate accepting things from my grandfather, but I accepted this, mostly for Reese. He would've had a fit if I declined this suite. I lock the door and head to my room. The view of the city is breathtaking, almost unreal. I sit at my desk and pull up the video again. I watch it repeatedly. This video was taken today. I can tell because I'm wearing my blue Nike long sleeve, my gray Nike sweatpants, and my white Nike shoes. I love anything Nike. After committing to this college, I got so many sponsorships my freshman year, and Nike was one of them. I'm worried that someone is watching me. I'm not sure why. My mom says people can be envious and hateful.

But who would be jealous of football? This thing going on feels personal, maybe a crush or something. I wanted to call Brooklyn about it, but it would just make her worry, and she has enough on her plate now. The time is 4:30 p.m. I figured I should get a nap since I don't have practice today. I pray that Reese remembers his keys today, so he doesn't wake me up.

Sure enough, Reese forgot his keys. At 6:30 p.m., I hear banging on the door. It scared the hell out of me. But, sure enough, it's Reese with his dramatics.

"Dylan, Nick was a sweetheart today," he said, walking in with a smile. This was hard to believe because Reese is always heartbroken over something Nick says or does. Nick is one of those guys who's not out of the closet and doesn't make it his personality. He's pretty low-key and chill, but Reese is the opposite. He's got a lot of personality and loves to argue over petty things. This is why he and Nick break up every other week. Then their "love" is rekindled with a hookup or an emotionless apology. I hate that Reese has to go through that type of toxic stuff, but he seems not to mind it as much anymore.

"So did Nick apologize for the argument last week?" I said, crossing my arms.

"Not necessarily; we just went to his room and—" Reese said, but I stop him before he finishes his thought.

"I don't need the details, Reese," I said, rolling my eyes. Reese overshares his "moments with Nick" a bit too much sometimes.

"Anyway, I have no plans tonight because my best friend is a total stay-at-home person," Reese said.

I shake my head. "I told you I didn't like parties." I shrugged.

"Okay, grandma," Reese said, rolling his eyes.

I laugh. I just can't seem to take him seriously when he's frustrated.

"I'm surprised Brooklyn's not over here," he said.

"Well, she's in the lab tonight; she wanted to finish some research before her midterms next week," I said.

"I never understood smart people," Reese said, shrugging his arms. He walks to the kitchen; I'm guessing to make spinach salad or that nasty kale smoothie thing he loves.

I get a text. No surprise, it's an unknown number again. It's another attachment, a picture. It's like the person is looking through the windows of the research lab, and there's Brooklyn alone looking into the microscope. I always tell Brooklyn to never stay alone, especially at night. She's so independent and hates having someone with her. I probably seem like an overprotective boyfriend, but I know the way other guys probably think when they see a girl alone. Plus, Brooklyn and I watch these horror movies she likes, which you would think would make her more cautious, but she thinks she's invincible. I grab my jacket and my keys.

"Where are you going?" Reese asked.

"Got to go see Brooklyn," I said as I walked out.

Chapter Two

Brooklyn Reed
Monday, October 31st, 7:00 p.m.

The lab is much quieter at night. It gives me a chance to collect samples without any interruption or distraction. Suddenly, the door flings open. There's Dylan standing in the doorway, like he's seen a ghost.

"Are you okay, Brookie?" he said with so much concern in his voice.

"Yeah, I'm fine. Are you okay?" I say this with a bit of sarcasm.

"I'm serious; did anyone come in here? Did you see anyone?" he said in a panicked voice.

"Dyl, you're the only person who's come in here," I said as I put my microcentrifuge tubes in the tray.

He sighs and walks up to hug me.

"What's going on?" I asked.

"It's just dark out, and you were gonna have to walk all the way across campus alone," he responded.

I have never seen Dylan like this. He's always calm or laughing at some bad joke. He seemed different, like he was scared.

"Come on; let's get you out of here," I say as I'm cleaning up the table. We head out into the dark courtyard. I feel Dylan's hand hold tightly to mine.

"Please stop going out at night by yourself. I worry," he said quietly.

"Okay, from now on, I won't go out alone, I promise," I said.

Dylan's always wanting to walk with me at night. He's so worried about me being alone. This is understandable, but he's busy, so I try not to bug him to walk with me, especially if he has practice. I tell him all the time that I can take care of myself, but he doesn't feel like I can. It's frustrating, but, like I said, I get it. I understand his worry. Maybe it's because I'm stubborn. At least that's what he says.

We get to my apartment on campus, and he walks me into the lobby. Then the elevator, then to my door.

"Do you want to come in?" I asked.

"I'll let you get some rest; just promise me, you won't go anywhere else tonight." Dylan said.

"I promise," I said.

He kisses my forehead and says, "Goodnight, I love you."

"I love you too," I say. I walk in, and Mariah's doing what she does best, watching soap operas. I never understood her fascination with them. They go on for years with zero development in the storyline. She's sitting on the couch with a blanket, and she's wearing a pink pajama set. She only wears sets; she refuses to sleep in anything else. Her dark brown hair is pinned up in a clip, and she has on those gold under eye patches. She says they help with eye bags and that I should "invest" in some. It's around 8:00 p.m. I'm debating if I want to go to bed early or get a jump start on the dishes before I forget about them. I always try to get everything done by Friday. That's the day Dylan has his games. I love watching him play. He's so happy. He's in his element when he's out on that field.

"Can you make a pizza or something? I haven't eaten all day," said Mariah.

"Haven't you learned your lesson with all that processed food?" I said.

Every time she eats frozen pizza, she throws up, which isn't surprising. Those things are disgusting, especially if they're not made properly, which when she makes them, they aren't. She and Dylan have such a similar taste in foods, and Reese and I can't stand it. Still, I preheat the oven and get the pepperoni pizza out. I'm trying to hold in my vomit at this point.

Mariah walks over to the kitchen and says, "Enough of the dramatics; they don't taste that bad." "That bad" was an understatement.

I head to the bathroom and prepare a shower. I like to take very hot showers. It's so relaxing, and I forget about how hectic life is for a minute. Except this time, I'm not as relaxed as I like to be. I can't stop thinking about Dylan. I have never seen Dylan shaken up like that. Dylan is an open book. His face will tell you a thousand words about his feelings without him having to open his mouth.

Chapter Three

Nick made me feel so important. But he could take away that feeling even faster now. I know I'm not exactly innocent in this situation, but I have never acted on these temptations. I'm a theatrical type of person if you will. I'm very dramatic, and I have a complex personality. Nick doesn't. I mean sure—he's so funny and can make anyone laugh, but behind his jokes, there's not a lot of depth there. There's a man with beautiful gray eyes who is tall, has brown hair, and has a muscular build. And it's odd because it's like a traditional jock who's reserved, dating a queer who's so out and proud. I'm not saying Nick is ashamed of his sexuality, but he's not as open about it as I am. He's bisexual, so I feel like sometimes I'm competing with both genders to get his attention. I like to be shown off, you know? I like being affectionate in public. He likes to keep this "lowkey," he says. But one thing I won't do is argue with him about that topic. It's hard to be an open homosexual male. I mean, sure, we live in New York City—the city filled with representation of our community—but that doesn't change the minds of everyone. I could be walking down the subway, and someone will yell out "twink" or "faggot," which doesn't hurt as much as it used to. I feel like Nick struggles with this part. He doesn't fit the gay stereotype. He's athletic. He's a flirt with everyone, even girls, which makes me nervous since he's not out yet.

"What's going on in your mind?" Nick asked.

"Long day, I guess," I said quietly.

He laughs. "Reese, it's only morning; what's your day like?" he said.

I sigh. How can I tell him I don't feel as happy as I want to? "Not much planned; might go to the art hall," I said. I love the art hall. It's filled with people like me.

Sometimes I still can't believe Nick is with me. I mean, sure, I act confident and prance around like a Kardashian, but I don't always feel this way. Maybe my overexaggerated personality is a mask for my own insecurities. Will I ever admit this to anyone? Heck no, I couldn't ever. Nick's talking, but I'm so caught up in my mind to even understand what he's saying.

"Reese, Reese?" he said gradually getting louder.

"Yeah," I responded.

"I'm going to training. Wanna meet tonight at my place?" he asked.

"Of course," I say. Nick was good at making me forget why I doubted him. Maybe to him, our relationship is only seen as sexual and nothing else. He won't talk to me all day sometimes, but then booty calls me at night. Don't get me wrong; I have absolutely no complaints. But sometimes I just want more from him—more love, less sex. Nick leaves and walks to the athletic building.

In the distance, I see Dylan and Brooklyn walking towards the science building. I would never admit this to Dylan, but I'm so jealous of their relationship. I mean, they are just so happy together. Dylan still talks about Brooklyn the same way he did when they first started dating.

"Hey, boo," said Mariah. She sits down right beside me and starts putting on her red lipstick, which looks beautiful with her brown skin.

"Hey," I said.

"Oh, Reese! What happened? Is it Nick?" she asked.

I take a deep breath and try to soak up the tear that's about to fall down my cheek, but it's followed by more tears.

Mariah digs in her Louis Vuitton bag and gives me a tissue. "Come on; what do we always say, Reese?" she said.

"Crying is for ugly people," I said with a slight laugh.

"Tell me what's going on," she said with concern.

"I just wish I could talk to Nick more about how I feel. It feels like maybe he's ashamed of me and doesn't want me in the ways I want him." I said.

"Oh, stop it. Nick's crazy about you," she said. She was right; Nick always talks to me with interest, but his actions don't match his words.

"I guess; I'm not sure he's as open as I am," I said as the hour bell chimes loudly.

"I've got fashion merchandise, but please, let's meet later so we can talk more about this. I hate seeing you upset," she said as she hugged me.

If anything, Mariah helps me the most with advice when it comes to Nick. I mean, I'd love to talk to Dylan about the way Nick makes me feel, but Dylan would probably punch him and ask questions later. Dylan was always protective over me, ever since high school when I came out. Dylan was always taller and muscular, so those scrawny guys never even made eye contact with me again. That's when Dylan and I became best friends. He kept the homophobes in check and even talked my parents out of sending me to "a camp for little boys who like to wear makeup and dresses." My parents still don't understand me, but they make an effort, and I have Dylan to thank for that.

Chapter Four

Mariah Parker
Tuesday, November 1st, 11:00 a.m.

I hated leaving Reese like that. He deserves so much better than what he receives. But deep down, I feel like Nick really does care about him; he just doesn't know how to show it. Like when Brooklyn first started dating Dylan, she was scared to love him. She's been through so much, and there's still so much she hasn't told me about her past. But I remember telling Dylan to be patient with her and she'd come around, and she did. Maybe I should say something to Nick? It could do more harm than good, but maybe it could help. I'm supposed to be walking to business management, but a friend needs me, so I do what I do best. Stay in everyone else's business.

I walk into the athletic building, heading straight to the weight-lifting room. There's Nick talking to their coach. He looks right at me, and deep down inside, he must know why I'm here. He ends his conversation and walks over to me.

"Mariah," he said while crossing his arms.

Nick and I never got along, per se. He knows I don't like him.

"We need to talk," I said, crossing my arms as well.

"About what?" He shrugged.

"About your boyfriend," I say.

He looks at me, then looks around. "What about him?" he asked.

I sigh. "I don't like the way you treat him, Nick," I say.

Nick had a tendency to get squirmy when talking about Reese. He'd get sort of nervous. I know deep down he has such strong feelings for Reese. Hell, I see it, but still, he needs to hear what I say.

"Listen, Nick; I'm not here to bitch at you or argue. I want you to hear me out." I say.

"Alright," he sighs.

"You know how deeply Reese feels for you. He's in love with you, and you aren't reciprocating that energy. I mean, I see the way you look at him. You care about him, but your actions fail to show that you care about him," I said.

He sighs and says, "I'm trying, okay? I care about Reese so much; I mean, he's the first guy I liked. He wants everyone to know we're together or that I'm—you know."

"That you're what, Nick? Say it out loud. It's not a bad word," I explained.

"You know how it is being out in this world. Once you say it, you can't take it back," Nick said.

"Nick, I know you're still coming to terms with who you are, but you guys have been together for more than six months. Don't pull him back into the closet with you. If you've heard the stories of how hard it was for Reese to come out. You'd know how bad your mentality is for him. How you make him feel wrong or make him question himself," I say.

Nick looks right at me and doesn't say a word. He knows I'm right. He knows that he's holding Reese back, but not in a good way.

"I gotta go; coach wants us on the field," Nick said as he jogs off.

Another talk with Nick that did absolutely nothing. It's like I'm talking, but in his mind, it's just white noise.

Chapter Five

Dylan Spencer
Tuesday, November 1st, 3:00 p.m.

I hate Tuesdays. Every Tuesday at 3:00 p.m., my family insists on having a family lunch. My mom, Alicia, she's amazing and my little sister Evie, who's too young to understand why I can't stand being around our grandfather. My dad, Nathaniel, is cool too. He's a surgeon, so he travels a lot to do procedures. He's different from my mom; he was never really the loveable kind. He never said how much he loved anyone.

My grandfather, the President of Morrid University, lives in the biggest housing establishment on campus. A big white house with a white fence. I always hated coming here, especially as a kid. The way he treated my grandmother was awful. When she passed, he got even worse. Gambling, drinking, and illegal investments. Of course, he'd pay off the press to keep our family's image clean.

"Dylan," my little sister, comes running to hug me.

"Evie, you're getting so big," I say.

I hate how big our age gap is. Evie's five, so I can't really see her grow up as much as I want to because of school and football. Evie loves Brooklyn so much, almost as much as I do. She always asks me to bring Brooklyn, but I'm embarrassed because of the way my grandfather acts sometimes. I always sit in between Evie and my mom. I smell alcohol, so I know who's here. It's the man of the hour, my grandfather, Marcus. Walking beside him is his young wife, Elaine, who's young enough to be his daughter. She's tall, lean, has black hair and brown eyes. Sitting next to my mom is my father, then Evie, and then me. Across the table are Marcus and Elaine. Marcus is known for his racist remarks that he tries to cover up with a grin. My mom has received some of the worst racist remarks from him. My mom's Cuban, so her skin is darker, her eyes are hazel, and her hair is dark brown. I look at my mom, Alicia, and she smiles at me and nods.

"Marcus, I'd like to pay my own rent now," I said.

His smile fades away slowly. "What's the point of that, Dylan?" he asked.

"Don't need you to pay my rent when I can pay it myself," I explained.

"Ungrateful, but have it your way," he said, putting rice on his plate.

"I can assure you he is grateful; he's just ready to be independent. Nothing is wrong with that," my mom said. She's always helping me when it gets like this because she knows I hate confrontations with Marcus.

"So how is your season going so far, Dylan?" asks Elaine.

"Pretty good; I'm number one in the state," I said.

My mom smiles and says, "We're so proud of you, Dylan."

"Is the coach still letting you take it easy on your knee?" Dad asked.

"Yeah, he is," I answered.

My grandfather looks at me; he hates when the attention isn't on him, so I knew he was going to say something now. "You know, Dylan, I never got a thank you for getting you into this university," he said.

"You know you didn't get me into this school. I did it on my own; my stats and my grades got me here, not you," I said, with frustration.

He laughs. "You wish; you were barely D1 going into college."

I know he's lying. I get up, and I know I'm about to say something bad. So I look down at Evie, and she's eating rice, humming a song, and completely oblivious to what's going on. I walk to the front door, unlock the car, and leave. I can't let Evie see that side of me, the side filled with anger.

I get a call from Brooklyn.

I answer, and she said, "Hey, how was your lunch?."

"Terrible like always, but hearing your voice makes my day better though," I said.

"I'm glad. How's my girl Evie? Is she still growing up so fast?" she asked.

"Unfortunately, yes; every time I see her, she gets bigger. She's good though, and she misses you,." I said.

"You know I can handle the things your grandfather says; it doesn't bother me," she said. But I can tell she doesn't mean it.

"It bothers me though," I say. I hear her sigh; she understands how terrible he is but still makes an effort to know my family. Her family lives in Florida, so she doesn't get to see them often. It's just her mom and her brother. Her nana lives in Florida too, but by herself. A few years ago, Brooklyn's grandpa passed away. I know she really loved him. She'll tell me stories about him and how he'd sneak her Snicker bars sometimes and tell her these scary stories. She says her grandpa was her best friend. I wish I got to meet him; he seemed like an amazing guy. I still don't know much about her dad, but I try not to bring him up.

"I'm with Reese right now. He said Nick was gonna stay the night at y'all place."

I know what that means so I ask, "Do you think I can stay with you tonight?."

"Of course," she said.

Tuesdays usually drain me, but today I was more exhausted than usual. I have practice in a few minutes, so I head to the locker room to get my pads. In walks Michael. Michael is one of the few guys on the team who are tolerable and cool. I tried to set him up with Mariah, but it didn't work out. I open my locker to put my phone in there, and there's a picture I look at every day of me and Brooklyn. Except, it's not in my locker.

"Who was in my locker?" I shout.

Everyone turns and looks at me.

"Wasn't me."

"I wouldn't do that."

"What happened?"

So many questions, yet no one was answering me. I put my pads on, slam my locker, and head out the door to get to the field. I hear footsteps follow closely behind me. It's Nick and Michael, the only guys on the team I'm close with.

"What happened?" asks Michael.

"You slammed your locker, so hard I feel like the floors moved," said Nick.

"Someone took something out of my locker," I say.

"You sure you didn't just take it out and put it somewhere else?" asks Nick.

"Now why would I ask you guys if I did it, Nick?" I say walking away.

Practice feels like forever. We run every single play for the game Friday until it's perfect. Practice gets over usually at six but the coach made us run because some freshman kept messing up the plays. So now it's around 7:15 p.m. I get into the locker room and open my locker. I get my phone, and there's an attachment from an unknown number. It's a picture of that missing photograph of me and Brooklyn. So it's clear this person has been in my locker.

"What the hell do you want?" I texted.

A few minutes go by, and they replied, "For you to understand, I can get to you whenever I want.."

Now I'm even more frustrated. This feels uncomfortable like they are stalking me or something. Then again, it could be someone's idea of a prank.

Chapter Six

Brooklyn Reed
Tuesday, November 1st, 9:30 p.m.

Dylan seemed more upset today. He deserves so much better than what he gets from his grandfather. I always wondered why bad things always happen to the best people. I try my best to be there for him. I offered to go with him a few times, even though I pray every time he doesn't let me. His grandfather pretty much disses him every chance he gets. His mom and his sister are amazing. His mom gets treated pretty badly too. He wasn't expecting his son to marry someone Cuban. Dylan doesn't look like you'd think he would. He has blonde, curly hair, blue eyes, and tan skin; he looks more like his father. But his sister Evie, who has light brown hair and golden eyes, looks more like their mom. I try not to push Dylan into talking about things with his family; he'll open up more about it when he's ready.

"Whatcha thinking about?" Mariah said as she looked over to me.

"Nothing much; just had a lot on my mind about this research stuff," I said.

"This is why you should have just been a fashion design major like me—not much work and lots of money,." she said.

I sighed. Mariah has no concept of money. I guess when you grow up rich, you don't really have to learn how to manage money. Not me, though; my dad left my mom when I was pretty young. He left us with absolutely nothing. My brother is older and wasn't around much, so it's always been my mom and me. So, needless to say, I really have to keep my grades up here if I plan to stay.

"Hello? Did you not just hear me?" Mariah shouted.

"What were you saying?" I asked.

"Would you match Gucci and Louis Vuitton? It feels wrong to do that," Mariah said.

"Who cares?" I say as I walk into my room. I wasn't trying to be mean; I just didn't care to hear about her rich people's problems. It gets to be too much sometimes. I couldn't shake this feeling I had about Dylan.

"Would he really lie to me?" I think to myself…Then I realized he would, especially to spare me the hurt I'd feel if I knew something. I don't think he's cheating or anything. I feel like it's something more. But, more like, what? I should give him a call to figure things out…

> Brooklyn: Hey, Dylan, what are you up to?
> Dylan: Lying here. Thinking.
> Brooklyn: Thinking about…?
> Dylan: Well, just the game this week. How's studying going?
> Brooklyn: Gave up, lying in bed.
> Dylan: Why's that? You always do homework on the couch.

Brooklyn: Not today. Mariah's out there designing something for fashion merchandise class.

Dylan: Ah, so you just needed some space from her crazy?

Brooklyn: Come on, Dyl, she's not that crazy.

Dylan: No, she is…

Brooklyn: Maybe. Is there anything you want to talk about?

Dylan: Nothing I can think of at this moment, beautiful.

Brooklyn: Oh, okay.

Dylan: Nick didn't end up coming over, so I'm about to sleep for a few; got so much to do tomorrow.

Brooklyn: Okay, night. Love you.

Dylan: Love you more, Brookie.

Nothing, absolutely nothing. I can't shake this feeling. Maybe it's nothing, and I'm just overthinking. Plus, Dylan would tell me if it was something serious…Wouldn't he?

Chapter Seven

I swear, I tossed and turned all night. Nick started acting differently again. Not answering my texts or my calls. He didn't even come over last night. I don't understand why I put up with this. I feel like I'm worth so much more than just hookups. I hate to do it, but I'm gonna have to talk to him. "Nick, meet me at Starbucks now," I texted him.

"Already in here. I see you."

I look up, and there he is. I'm guessing he just got back from lifting this morning.

He walks up to me. "Hey," he said.

"Do you think we can actually have a conversation, or are you gonna ignore me?" I asked with my arms crossed.

He sighs and looks upset that I said that. "You know how I feel about you; why do you have to complicate it?" he asked.

I'm thinking to myself—how in the hell am I the one complicating stuff? All I ever wanted was for him to show me he cared about me.

"Nick, you don't care about me," I said.

"How could you even say something like that?" he responded.

"Cause it's true, Nick; I'm over feeling like this," I say, slightly in anger.

Nothing. Nick says nothing. He's just looking at me and around us.

"Unbelievable," I say under my breath.

"Reese, venti iced caramel macchiato with light foam," the Starbucks worker announces.

I get my coffee, and I walk out. Now I'm upset though, and I have an urge to cry or shout or something, but I can't do it in public.

It's 9:45 a.m., there I am, in an art seminar, painting black lines everywhere. Mariah walks in; I swear this girl is never where she's supposed to be.

"Are you feeling, okay?" she asked with concern. "You hate dark colors, Reese. Talk to me," she said. She does sound genuine.

"Broke up with Nick," I said.

"That explains why he was bitching in math this morning. He's been snappy to everyone," she said.

That would've meant he would have cared, right? He didn't seem too bothered when I mentioned how frustrated I was... speak of the devil.

"Now he's calling me," I say as I roll my eyes. I get up and walk outside the classroom.

Nick: Reese?

Reese: What?

Nick: I'm sorry, okay? I didn't mean to hurt you.

Reese: Hmmm, then why do you keep hurting me?

Nick: It's not my intention. I don't know how to deal with this stuff.

Reese: Deal with what, Nick? Enlighten me.

Nick: This liking guy's thing. It's new, okay? This is scary.

Reese: I know, Nick, but you can't pull me down with you. It's like you're ashamed of who you are.

Nick: Maybe I am. Maybe I don't want it to be this way.

Reese: You can't change who you are, Nick. If you don't accept yourself, do you really think other people will?

Nick: I don't know why you are pressing this topic. Can we just drop it?

Reese: No, you've got to figure that out.

Nick: I want to be with you, Reese, but how can I really fix this?

Reese: By being yourself and stop treating me like I'm some parasite.

Nick: I'm sorry.

Reese: Are you?

Nick: More than I can express.

Reese: Do you even want this to work?

Nick: Yes, and it will.

Reese: How?

Nick: Can you come to the hallway?

I walk to the hallway. There he is. Standing there.

"I'm sorry. Give me another chance?" he asks. "I'll show you how serious I am about us, okay?" he said. "I don't want to lose you. Please give me another chance".

I guess I really can't stay mad at him. He seemed to mean it this time. "I forgive you, but this is the last time, Nick; I can't keep doing this with you," I explained.

"You won't have to; I'll work on it," he explained.

Chapter Eight

Mariah Parker
Wednesday, November 2nd, 11:30 a.m.

Seeing how Nick was willing to apologize to Reese made so much sense. I knew Nick was capable of some good. I still don't like him too much, but he's made progress, which counts for something. In the cafe, I see Brooke. She's reading a book like always.

"What are you plotting?" said Michael as he walks up to me. Michael Taylor. A football player who is ironically an English major. He's who Dylan tried to set me up with. The thing is the date wasn't awful; he was just too invested in learning more about me. There wasn't even much about me to tell. I'm a twenty-one-year-old fashion design major. I grew up in Boston with my parents who are lawyers. I went to a boarding school all of high school. Should I have told him about this one time when my dad took me to this waffle place and I tried peanut butter waffles and my face swelled up and I was rushed to the hospital? Or about how I wish my parents would've spent more time with me growing up? How having a nanny was cool but upsetting when I saw my nanny more than my own parents. No, he didn't need to know that stuff about me. Why would he? Would he even care? It's not that I didn't trust Dylan's capabilities to find me a guy; I just don't trust anyone.

"You never called me back," Michael said.

"There was a reason for that," I said as I walked away. I find Brooklyn and Dylan sitting down together, and I join them.

"Hey, Mariah," they said, almost at the same time.

"Hey, you guys." I said.

"So was Michael still annoying? He keeps talking about you," said Dylan.

I roll my eyes. "We went out once. Can he just let it go already?" I complain.

"He seems nice, Mariah; you could at least let him down gently," said Brooke.

"Does everyone just think I'm awful here?" I ask defensively. They would be right. I have been awful to him. I shouldn't take my own frustration out on him. I never really learned how to talk about how I felt. Whenever I'd cry, dad would just give me his platinum card and tell me to spend as much as I wanted to. I would've liked talking about how I felt. Maybe I would be nicer now. Less hostile and more open. *Ding Ding*. I always hated Dylan's ringtone; it's so loud for no reason. Lately, he's been so jumpy; I'm not sure if Brooklyn has noticed yet, but it's sort of obvious. I don't want to mettle, but something feels wrong. Dylan's one of those guys who pretty much always has his shit together, or at least seems to. It doesn't seem like he does anymore. I wanted to ask Brooke about it, but I don't think it's truly my place. Dylan gets up to check his phone, but he seems different when he comes back, almost like he saw a ghost.

"I'll catch up with you guys later. I got some stuff to handle," said Dylan.

"Everything okay?" Brooke asked.

"Yeah, just some family stuff," he said as he kissed her cheek. Then he's gone.

I couldn't hold it in any longer. "Brooklyn, why is he acting so weird all of a sudden?" I asked.

She shrugs.

"So, you don't know what he's up to at all?" I asked.

"No, Mariah, and truthfully, it's none of my business unless he tells me," said Brooklyn as she sips her water.

Chapter Nine

Dylan Spencer
Wednesday, November 2nd, 12:15 p.m.

In a lot of ways, I feel stuck. These texts have been happening for around two days now. I've been getting sneaky messages like this all year, but I just ignored it. Before, it felt like just some clingy college girl stuff. But now, it feels like so much more than that. I was sitting in the cafe with Brooklyn and Mariah, and I got another message. It was weird. That picture I was looking for in my locker? Well, I got another picture of it from an unknown number. Not only did it bother me because someone went into my personal space, but what frustrated me the most was that Brooklyn's face was crossed out. Now anyone can tell you that I protect that girl with everything in me. I would do anything to keep her safe. The list of people who could've done this is slim. Not even my own teammates know my locker code; not even the coaches know it. Each athlete has a contract signed where no one can access their locker unless there's suspicion of drugs or drug enhancers. None of the athletes here used enhancers, that I knew of. All athletes are tested for steroids almost every month.

Nick: Dylan ,what do you have going on?

Dylan: Trying to figure out who is messing with me.

Nick: What do you mean?

Dylan: Oh, it's nothing; just wondering who had been in my locker.

Nick: That thing is still missing?

Dylan: Yeah. Not sure who's got it.

Nick: I can ask around if you want. I doubt it's anybody on the team.

Dylan: Yeah, me too.

Nick: You talked to Reese today?

Dylan: No, haven't seen him; been busy. What's up?

Nick: Well, I apologized and told him I wanted things to work.

Dylan: Well, don't you say that every time?

Nick: Point is, I mean it this time. I really do.

Dylan: How'd you get him to forgive you?

Nick: Well, I skipped lifts and surprised him in class.

Dylan: Wow. That's surprising coming from you.

Nick: Yeah, yeah. I'll catch you later, man. I'm headed to lifts since I missed earlier. Which is where you should be too.

Dylan: Not going today. Got a bad cramp.

Nick: Gotcha. Catch you later.

Dylan: Alright.

I knew what I had to do, so I was headed to do so. I went to New York City's best computer guy I knew. His name is

Lucas Carter. I had a class with Lucas my sophomore year. He always had a sense of familiarity, but I could never remember where I knew him from. It's no secret that he doesn't like me too much. He puts all athletes in some bubble, as if all of us are bad people. I get that the rest of the team has some guys who are just like the narrative he's portraying, but it's not me. I walk into Johnson's computer building. It's filled with state-of-the-art technology. When you look up at the ceiling, you can see the sky. The ceiling is glass, which is cool. I walk up the stairs right to the office with the darkest lighting. I just knew it was his office. I knock on the door and peek my head in.

Lucas spins his rollie chair around, and I see the disgust as his eyes meet mine. "Oh, it's you," he said.

I walk in, and I shut the door behind me. "Listen, Lucas, I know you don't like me too much, but I need a favor, and it's going to sound crazy," I said.

"Dylan Spencer, 3.7 GPA, 6'3", and rich," he said with disgust.

I'm not sure why he said all that; it literally had nothing to do with anything. I roll my eyes. "I'm not here to entertain your bigotry, Lucas; I really need your help," I said.

"Take a seat, tell me," he said. I sighed.

"This is going to sound crazy; I know it is, but someone's stalking me and harassing me, and I can't figure out where the messages are coming from. Could you please trace this unknown number?" I say with desperation.

"You know it's gonna cost you; this type of project could take me weeks," he said.

"Name your price," I said.

"250," he said with a big smile.

"I should have figured you would charge me. But it's important I find this person," I said. I hand him my phone, and he looks at it.

"Give me four weeks to figure this out. I should be able to get this done. But you have to understand this is an unknown number; they could be using a burner phone," he explains.

"Any bit of information could help me," I said.

"Here, use this until you get yours back," he said as he handed me an iPhone.

"It's an extra phone I had been working on. I've installed a lockdown; only saved numbers can call or message, and I can wire it through this computer if you still want it tracked for safety reasons..." he said.

"Yeah, man, thank you so much. I appreciate it," I said.

"Yeah, of course. Stay safe out there. Looks like I've got a new project," he said.

"Alright, catch you later," I said as I walked out. I'm not sure how quickly he can get this done, but if I can at least find the area where the texts are coming from, that helps a lot.

Once again, late to global studies. Professor Gwen is such a nag, I swear. I'm debating if I should even go into this class, but I have nothing else to do. I walk into the class, and there she is standing up at the smart board sipping her coffee, which I'm sure she got earlier this morning. I look directly at her, and she doesn't say a word. I take my seat in the corner and take out my MacBook Pro. I checked my email, and there's an attachment of photographs. I click on the link, and I see a bunch of photographs of Brooklyn. Pictures similar to the ones of me. She's not aware the pictures are being taken. There are pictures of her in the lab, at Starbucks, and even at other spots on campus. Not sure what this person's end goal is. It's unfair to me, and now they're targeting Brooklyn, who is too oblivious to the dangers. I still don't understand why she goes out by herself. She is not invincible at all. Now I'm worried about her being alone. But if I suddenly ask to go everywhere with her, she's gonna know something is wrong, and she's going to get sick of me for sure. I want to know how I can keep a close eye on her without being too overbearing. The only person I can think of who is close to her, and it wouldn't be too suspicious, is if I told Mariah. Despite how snarky Mariah is, I believe she would stay by Brooklyn as much as she could without it being too obvious. Now I've got to tell Mariah...

Dylan: Mariah, hey?

Mariah: Hello.

Dylan: I got to tell you something, but you cannot tell Brooklyn.

Mariah: I knew you were cheating.

Dylan: What the hell? No.

Mariah: Then why have you been acting so sketchy?

Dylan: I have been keeping something. But this is so serious, Mariah. It's dangerous.

Mariah: Interesting...Tell me more.

Dylan: Well, for the past two or so days. I've been getting these weird messages and such. I got a Dropbox sent to me of pictures of me, yet I had no idea the pictures were being taken. I've been getting weird messages along with that, like creepy texts. They broke into my locker at the gym and stole the picture I had of Brookie and me. Today, they sent pictures of Brooklyn.

Mariah: Wow...that's weird. Do you know why they're doing this?

Dylan: No, I don't. I'm having this guy named Lucas track the IP address and stuff, and he gave me a burner phone. He said no weird numbers could call me here.

Mariah: Yeah, I was wondering why the number was different.

Dylan: Mariah, I don't know what to do. They're targeting Brooklyn now. Just promise me that if anything happens to me, you'll protect her.

Mariah: I won't let her out of my sight, I promise.

Dylan: Thank you. I know if I come around more, she's gonna think I'm too protective again.

Mariah: But Dylan? What are you gonna do? What if this escalates more?

Dylan: Honestly, Mariah. I have no idea what to do...

Chapter Ten

Brooklyn Reed
Wednesday, November 2nd, 1:05 p.m.

Research was always such a big part of my life. I had my whole life planned out at such a young age. I wanted to help people. I knew no matter what I did in this life, I just wanted to make a difference. I always thought I wanted to be a doctor. Now, I feel conflicted. Don't get me wrong; I love science, and I love the challenge of solving a stoichiometry problem in chemistry, but something feels like it's missing. I'm at the point now where I need to find a focus, whether I want to go to med school or not. It's junior year, and it's almost the end of the semester. I'm conflicted on what to do. I have my meeting with my adviser soon. He's gonna ask me so many questions, and I'm not going to know what to answer with. I can graduate in the spring if I want too because I have so many credits. I really want to talk to Dyl about it, but he's been so in his own head about things. I don't really know what's been going on with him lately, but, I'm just gonna hope everything is okay.

My mom's been doing well; she's thinking of moving from Florida to be closer to me. My mom's the strongest person I know. I wouldn't be here if she didn't encourage me every day. She's my biggest supporter, and she's believed in me at times where I did not believe in myself. Sometimes I wonder how I even ended up at Morrid University. This school's tuition is insane. It's about 74,000 a year, and they hardly give out scholarship money. I had to bust my ass to get here—practically acing every single class in high school and every standardized test.

I was six when my parents got divorced. It was a messy year; it was filled with heartbreak and disappointment. What hurt the most was how quickly my dad just left. He practically abandoned us. He took the house and all the money in the divorce. We had to move into an apartment that year. The big two-story house with the playroom was no longer home. I didn't even know what to call home.

My brother, Myles, was always interested in music. He was always playing some instrument for as long as I can remember. Just him in his room and music playing. I guess that's where my inspiration for music came from. Being so young and watching him play all these instruments inspired me. He and I have a big age gap. He was around thirteen when I was born. He was always so protective over me, and him being older definitely made it worse when I started to date. My earliest memory of my brother was when I was about three or four. I was always playing with some type of Barbie doll, and he would just be in his room. I remember being in the playroom and hearing him play all types of things, from rock to jazz to classical. He would always play the saxophone. I always wanted to be as talented as him, so when I got older, I started taking violin lessons. That was the only instrument he didn't learn, but I got the idea of it pretty quickly. So, when my brother got older, he wanted to go to college to study music and the arts. He got into Julliard, which is a very impressive school and one of the best for the arts. Unfortunately, he couldn't go. He ended up not being able to go to college at all because we couldn't afford it, and Julliard doesn't give many scholarships. My father didn't help him much either. I guess that's why my mom did everything she could for me to be able to go to college. My goal is to become so financially wealthy that I can just buy her a big house and whatever car she'd like. There's nothing I could do to repay the sacrifices she's made for my brother and me. Sometimes I feel so alone with this. My friends here just wouldn't understand because they came from money. Me, on the other hand…I have to work my butt off to even be able to stay here. I believe Dylan is very humble about everything he has. He has always been that way.

I met Dylan my freshman year at orientation. I talked to him for the first time that same day at the study abroad table. I was looking at the pamphlet for Cuba.

He said to me in Spanish, "My mother is Cuban. She said she wanted to take me to Cuba one day with my sister to see old Havana." I turned to the side and saw a blue-eyed, curly-headed blonde boy. I was so surprised because his Spanish sounded so authentic. I guess he was used to the surprised look people had when he spoke in Spanish.

He laughed and said, "My mom's language is Spanish, and she taught me at a young age; it's sort of just stuck with me, and it's how we talk bad about my grandpa in front of him."

I laughed, and I took a good look at him. "You said your mom is Cuban? Tell me more," I say.

"Well, she moved to America when she was sixteen with my abuela. She promised one day that she'd take my sister and me there. She loves Old Havana in Cuba. She says it's important to know the history there. She says, gazing up at the grand Baroque and neoclassical buildings, that it's easy to imagine what life in Cuba was like two hundred years ago," he explained.

I could tell he deeply cared about his mom and liked to learn about her. Something about him seemed so genuine; he had this light in his eyes, which was something I had never seen in anyone before. Dylan was respectful and maintained eye contact so well that, in a way, it made me nervous. Not a bad nervous, but an exciting one. We kept talking for a while, and his grandfather walked by. He looked so shaken up around him, and I could see that light in his crystal blue eyes just dim a bit. It's like when you have a night light and you cover it with your hands to see how dark it'll be without it. That day, I knew there was something special about him. We exchanged numbers and just kept talking for a while. I didn't have an initial romantic thought about him; it was just wanting to know more about him. So time went by, and he asked me to be his girlfriend. I was hesitant at first because I had my own issues I hadn't really dealt with yet, but he made me feel safe enough to open my heart up to him. To this day, I still look at him the same way I did at orientation, in complete admiration, and wonder how I was able to get so lucky with him. The number of girls who try to get with him to this day is overwhelming. It makes me nervous sometimes because they are the opposite of me. Skinny, blonde girls with so much money. Dylan always assures me he would never give them the time of day regardless of what I have to say about it.

"Brooklyn," said Mariah.

I look around in confusion because why is she in the science building? "Mariah, what are you doing in here? You said this building gives you a headache," I said with a laugh.

"Well, it does; all the numbers and symbols everywhere. I just came to see you. I wanted to check in and see how you were doing today," she rambles.

"I'm fine, just doing some chemistry homework," I say.

"Need some help?" she asks.

I'm confused because she said that with such a straight face. Mariah is no student; she believes in wealth over knowledge.

"Are you okay? You never come to this building," I say.

"Ugh, I can't even check on my roomie anymore apparently," Mariah said, crossing her arms. "Well, of course, you can," I say.

"Okay, good," she said as she took a seat beside me on the couch and opened a magazine.

Chapter Eleven

Reese Woods
Wednesday, November 2nd, 4:30 p.m.

Nick wasn't the first guy to break my heart. My freshman year in high school, there was a guy named Kameron. He was tall and skinny, and he had this shortcut of black hair. The way he moved, the way he talked…Everything about him was majestic; I'm not even kidding. He was the most perfect boy you could even imagine. He was my first "boyfriend," or at least I believed he was. It was the night after the record-breaking basketball game of the season. Our school won by fifty points; twenty-three of the points were his. I was texting him for a while before that, but he wanted me to keep it a secret. At this point, I wasn't friends with Dylan yet. Dylan was the typical high school athlete; he played football and basketball. The point of being with Kameron was the fact that one knew about it. He didn't tell anyone, so I couldn't tell anyone either. My relationship with him was purely texting. It consisted of only that. That's not where things went wrong; although they should have been. I was okay with just a texting relationship. I knew he wasn't out yet and I wasn't either.

One day, it was the fourth period, around early afternoon. A text was sent, people's phones went off, and everyone secretly checked their phones. I didn't get the text though. You can guess what the text was. It was such a clique, but it happened. These were screenshots of Kameron and my messages. It was anonymous, so no one knew who the text came from. I was officially out as gay now, not by choice. I knew my life was going to be hell in that high school now. Only one person at that school knew I was gay. It was Kameron. The past few hours of that school day were absolute hell. I was thrown against lockers and treated horribly.

That's when I was blessed to meet Dylan. The guys on the team were hassling me in the locker room, and he stepped in. I had to talk him out of beating the shit out of Kameron. Trust me, I wanted him too, but Dylan wasn't a violent person. I had only seen him get angry over a few people. Those people are his mom, sister, Brooklyn, and me. He's a protector; he always has been. That's what I admire the most about him. You would think a boy with as much trauma as him would be a rude person. He's the opposite of it. He's a ray of sunshine usually. Seeing him obsess over Brooklyn has been the most beautiful thing I have witnessed. He's giving her his all, I swear. He tends to overthink sometimes with her.

Brooklyn may not think so, but she is stunning. She's one of the prettiest girls on our campus, effortlessly so. She hardly does her makeup, and her hair is usually in a slick back high ponytail, but she is still so pretty. I adore how clueless she is about her beauty. Brooklyn is the best girl out there for him.

Dylan's a sweetheart, but he has a lot of anger within himself. That anger stems from the abuse from his grandfather. Dyl said that ever since his grandmother died when he was little, his grandfather spiraled. His grandfather was drinking a lot, acting violent, and always angry. He used to take that frustration out on Dylan. He would grab him or scuffle him really bad. I guess that's why Dylan got so big. He really buffed up our freshman year. His grandfather always lived here in New York but had a house in Pennsylvania. We used to live in Pennsylvania. Dylan would come to school with these bruises, and one time he had a cut on his hand. I never questioned him about it, but I had a pretty good idea of where it came from. Dylan's mom had no idea, I'm sure. Dylan's dad knew, though, but he was never home much.

Chapter Twelve

Mariah Parker
Wednesday, November 2nd, 8:15 p.m.

've been sticking by Brooklyn's side all day. I think I took it too far when I tried to go with her to the bathroom. I'm sure she's confused. I just wish Dylan would just tell her what's going on, but he thinks it's safer this way. I love the relationship they have. I've never had that before, but I've sort of sworn off dating for a while. I haven't dated since my senior year of high school. I had known this guy for a while; we were on and off our sophomore year. I'll admit I never treated him the best that year, but what he put me through isn't even comparable. My best friend at the time was named Avery. She was in an economics class with this guy. She told him I thought he was cute, and I wanted to give it another go. He was surprised I was still interested in him, so he texted me. We started to talk more. I was happy then, and I fell in love. The way I felt for him—I had never felt that way before with anyone. I started being so involved with him, sneaking out, lying about where I was going, and pushing my mom away when she wouldn't let me hang out with him at night. My mom always had a bad feeling about him. Said he would break my heart. I never listened; I should've though. This guy wasn't a perfect boyfriend toward the end of our relationship. He was in the beginning though, planned dates, wanted to meet my parents, opened the door for me, paid for my greasy fries, and gave me his all. But after a while, all of that changed. What seemed so perfect became so toxic so fast. He started being weary of my guy friends and wouldn't trust me around them. After the break-up, things just escalated more. He had an older brother that just made my life hell at school. It sucked a lot... Everyone thought his brother was probably obsessed with me. It started to seem that way too. Everything was always my fault, you know? Apparently, it was my fault he cheated too...After a while, I just became numb to it all. I didn't want to date again or ever put myself out there like that. Not that I was scared of being cheated on, but I was scared of the aftermath of it all. Maybe he would ruin my next relationship. Which was a fear I had on my own. I still haven't really coped with it all, I guess. It was a big enough issue that I even stopped going to school for a few days at a time. I was just scared too, I guess. I never got closure. So here I am, in my twenties, still afraid to love again. It's pathetic, I know, but I swear, I have this fear of putting myself out there again. I guess that's why I shut Michael out. I didn't want to lose myself again. You know what they say, you never forget your first love.

Chapter Thirteen

Dylan Spencer
Wednesday, November 2nd, 11:25 p.m.

The past few hours have been quiet. I have not received a text or email. Lucas has started working on my phone and says he'll keep me updated with anything he uncovers. Mariah has stayed with Brooke all day. I'm sure she's driving Brooklyn insane by now, either complaining about the sales this week or about how much work she has to do. I'm worried I may have waited too long to tell anyone. I mean, I've gotten weird messages ever since I got to this school, but these messages feel so much different. It feels almost like a warning or something that is supposed to keep me up at night. I'm not the type of guy to get spooked or worried like this, but it feels different now that Brooklyn is involved.

Nick came over tonight, and for the first time Reese didn't ask me to leave. I guess they have fixed their relationship to be more "romantic" rather than "intimate." I walked out to the living room, and they were laying there on the couch, cuddling. It was a weird sight, for sure. Something I really could have gone without seeing. Nonetheless, Reese looks happy, which is all I have ever wanted for him anyway. When I met Reese, I instantly knew he was gonna be my best friend and that I was gonna protect him. He was so broken when I met him, and I was too. I guess that's what made us bond quickly. He was the first to acknowledge my grandpa's abuse. I was pretty quiet about it, my dad noticed at one point so he'd stop sending me over there. It took him years but I guess I hid it pretty well. I was tired of being so weak and couldn't fight back. So freshman and sophomore year, I really hit the gym. I worked out every morning from five to seven. I was benching, lifting and running. Everything you could possibly imagine. After my grandpa decided to move back to New York, I had already become pretty big. I was taller and stronger than him. He knew I wasn't defenseless anymore, and I could fight back. It wasn't the best feeling to know that was the only way to escape it, but it helped me later on with sports in high school. I always protect Evie too. I told Mom to never send her over to Marcus's house, especially not alone. I always wished my dad was around more. He was home more when I was younger, but not much in high school. I always wished he would tell me he was proud of me. But he doesn't talk much. I guess he is his father's son. I guess I can't blame him for being that way.

I decided to go on my computer for a bit. Check my stats, emails, and stuff. So, I reached in my bag, to which I saw this note.

Dear Dylan Spencer,
I understand you may not know me, and you're probably wondering how the hell this letter got in your bookbag. I can't tell you my name; it's for my own safety. I'm in your mass communications class; you went to sleep for a

bit, so I just slipped it in there when I walked by. A part of me wanted to just drop this and sweep it under the rug but I haven't been able to sleep or eat for weeks. I have no one else to turn to, but a part of me believes you're someone worth trusting with this information. Your grandfather, the president of this campus, sexually assaulted me my freshman year. I'm currently a sophomore here at Morrid. This has been eating me up since it happened. I knew if I came forward no one would believe me; they'd say I was lying or just trying to get money. I was an intern in his office that year. I was thinking of becoming a law student, and he is a lawyer; well he was a lawyer before. So, I applied that fall and got accepted that spring. It started off small; he'd say flirty things or compliment my eyes. It was nothing that concerned me too much at first, then it escalated. He constantly wanted me to stay late, and he'd say things about how short my skirt was. To which I ignored these comments and would just go back to work. Until one night, I stayed till around nine. The office was empty that night…I heard the door lock and turned around, and he was standing there. I'm not even sure why I'm telling you this, but I need someone to believe me. I have no one; my parents live far away, and I'm originally from Cuba. I have no one here. I can't go home because my visa won't allow me to come back to the States if I do. Please believe me; please help me. I'm willing to meet to discuss this, but I must know that I can trust you. You cannot tell anyone. Promise me that. If you find it in your heart to believe me, here's my number— to a burner, of course. (646)-795-8238. Text me, and we can find a time to meet.

My initial reaction was shock. Was someone telling me this is what happens behind closed doors here? Unfortunately, this isn't even the first time I've heard something like this. So, I believe her; she sounds terrified, but my grandfather causes that effect in people. I know she needs someone, a friend. She needs Brooklyn. I would have Mariah talk to her maybe since Mariah knows how deep this situation is, but this is something Brooklyn would be good at talking to her about. So, I have to tell Brooklyn. Well, tell her parts of it.

Dylan: Hey.

Brooklyn: Hey, what's up?

Dylan: Do you think maybe you can talk for a bit?

Brooklyn: Talk about what?

Dylan: Are you alone or not?

Brooklyn: Mariah's been more needy than normal.

Mariah: Hey, be nice.

Dylan: Well, ask her if you can be alone for a bit in your room. Need to talk to you. Tell her I need you alone.

Brooklyn: Leave Mariah; he needs to tell me something. He said to tell you.

Dylan: Is she still there?

Brooklyn: No, she left. What's up?

Dylan: Well, I want to tell you this in person. You think we can meet in the lobby of your building?

Brooklyn: Yeah, that sounds good. Let me know when you're here.

Dylan: Will do.

Chapter Fourteen

Brooklyn Reed
Thursday, November 3rd, 12:00 a.m.

'm worried about why he wants to meet so late. It's got to be something important. A few minutes go by, and he's here. I walk down to the lobby, and he's sitting in the corner chair, facing away from the cameras in the lobby. He's holding a paper. I look at him, walk towards him, and take a seat in the chair beside him.

"What's going on?" I said with concern. Dylan takes a deep breath and tells me about this girl, whom, his grandfather sexually assaulted…I'm speechless; I don't even know what to say. My heart breaks for her. I can't imagine how she even feels. She probably feels so powerless and scared. She has no one to turn to, and the person she fears is in power over her and everyone at this school.

"What can I do to help?" I asked.

"She doesn't trust anyone, Brookie. She's not gonna trust me. She needs a strong person, someone like you, a woman. I'm sure I'm gonna hurt her more because her abuser is my grandfather, and in a way, I'm related to him. I don't want to traumatize her anymore," Dylan explained.

"Let me text the number," I said.

12:30 a.m.

Brooklyn: Hello?

(646)-795-8238: Who's this?

Brooklyn: My name's Brooklyn. I'm Dylan's girlfriend.

(646)-795-8238: What did he tell you?

Brooklyn: He told me enough. Don't be mad at him. He just wanted you to have me to trust since he's a guy and his grandfather hurt you.

(646)-795-8238: How can you help me?

Brooklyn: Well, I can give you moral support, be a shoulder to cry on, and most importantly, help you get justice.

(646)-795-8238: How do I get justice? He's the president here.

Brooklyn: No one deserves to be assaulted. Most importantly, he deserves to pay for his actions. Dylan will help you in whatever way you need. But we want to be there for you.

(646)-795-8238: How?

Brooklyn: Well, it may not help much, but one of my very good friends back home was sexually assaulted by a coach, and she was able to get him locked away for good. It was a long and tiring process. I may not know what you have gone through, but I've seen firsthand how heartbreaking this is, and I want to be there for you.

(646)-795-8238: Thank you. I just would like to keep my identity a secret for now.

Brooklyn: Yes, that is perfectly fine. Now the first thing we have to do is find evidence, if you can find any. Of course, I believe you, but it's for the court. They're gonna ask.

(646)-795-8238: I have the underwear from that night. When I took it off, I put it in a Ziplock bag. Is that strong enough evidence?

Brooklyn: Yes, actually. Now hide it. Keep it safe. Now I want you to write a statement. A long statement of what happened. We will take it to the court office off campus.

(646)-795-8238: I will do that this week. Thank you both so much.

Brooklyn: We are here for you. This is my number, so if you need to talk or text with updates. Text or call here.

"Dyl, how do we help her?" I say. He looks at me. His eyes are pretty watery. "I hate she's had to go through that. No woman should have her body violated like that. We are taking Marcus down," Dylan said, and I can tell he means it.

Chapter Fifteen

Reese Woods
Thursday, November 3rd, 4:30 p.m.

Thursday, Mariah and I go into the city. Usually, we look at the sales to forget for a second that we have homework to be done. It's amazing how much is beyond the gates of the college. I would kill to have a life where all I do is come home to a good husband after a long day of shopping. Since I know the chances of that are slim, I have to think realistically.

"Mariah, I still don't know what I want to do with my life," I said.

"Why don't you design things? You like artsy stuff," she said.

Mariah was right. I loved to design. It was one of my favorite things to do, whether it was something interior or even designing clothes. I could never see anything coming out of it. Then suddenly, Mariah stops walking.

"Holy shit. I just had the best freaking idea in the history of ideas, Reese," she said, all giddy with a smile.

"Tell me the idea," I said.

"Imagine this…you and I have a fashion line. We could be the next Victoria Secret business…You design art for the clothing, and I stitch it, and we go from there," she said all in one breath. This girl was something, but damn was she brilliant.

"I am loving this idea 100 percent, but how do we even get started?" I ask. Opening a business wasn't easy. It would take time and lots of money. Although, those are both things Mariah and I have.

"I have a savings of $20,000…I always thought I'd use it for emergency purchases, but that's enough for a down payment on a business here in the city and rent," she said. "See, this building is empty. It's a decent size and located right in the heart of Manhattan," she said.

"Look, it has the number to call on here; Mariah, let's call it.," I said.

After calling the number, they wanted a down payment immediately, so we ran to the bank across the street and went to the place to give the money. Mariah was able to give enough money to put down the down payment and the first three months of rent. I have about $6,000 saved, which is enough to put toward materials. We wasted no time. That whole afternoon, we spent running up and down the city. We bought fabric, sketch pads, pencils, and snacks, and Mariah even spent $600 on two glass desks to put in the place.

"I have some sketches back at campus," I said.

"Let's head back to campus to get your sketches and get some more things," Mariah said. So, within a few minutes, we locked up and headed back to school.

Chapter Sixteen

Mariah Parker
Thursday, November 3rd, 9:45 p.m.

After Reese and my spur-of-the-moment decision, I was blessed enough to receive a call from my mother dearest, concerned why I accessed my savings. I told her the news, and immediately I was questioned.

"How do you expect this to work? How are you gonna manage this? How are you gonna be able to hand stitch clothing for every customer?"

They were silly questions; questions I had an answer to. I was a professional stitcher at best. I have always been good with a needle and thread, and I have invested in a sewing machine that can sew up to five things at once.

I was more than confident in Reese's designing abilities. He's so talented and someone I know I can rely on. I guess the decision was quick, but it was a good one. Plus, if it doesn't work, then it was a lesson, but I have a really good feeling about it.

"Can I take this off now?" asks Brooklyn as she tugs on her waistline.

I may have made her my little model. I needed a living body to put my clothes on, so I've had her stand still for about three hours. Some may call that Brooklyn abuse, but I don't care. I needed a human, and it allowed me to keep a close eye on her. Although I'm sure she's absolutely sick of me by now, I told her the good news about the business, and she was happy. I feel like this is the first time I've been excited about something in a really long time. I was never good at school; if anything, I sucked at it so much. I hated math, science, history, and all those other classes you have to study in. I always loved to sew. Ever since I was about seven years old, I was at my grandma's house, and she taught me how to hand stitch. It was so old school, but it was unique and something I started to do in my free time. By high school, I was designing my own clothes. Just about everything I wear is something I've designed or altered on my own. I enjoy the creativity of it and the freedom of being able to pick how I want something to look.

I know my parents were angry when I decided to major in fashion design. They expected me to be a lawyer like them, but the truth is, it was never something I was interested in. I couldn't study for anything to save my life, and I sure as hell wasn't interested enough in school to pursue something like that. I was always fashion smart, not book smart. It's not that I'm against it...well, actually I am. I guess that's why Reese and I connected so quickly. I met him my freshman year here. He was sitting in the arts hall, just sketching something. His art is so effortlessly beautiful. It could be something as simple as a sun, and it would be perfect. He could sketch as quickly as ever too, like, how does his mind just know what to do? Beats me, but both of us, as a team, would be unstoppable. He'd be the artist, and I'd be a handywoman. I would put everything together to make it work.

I'm exhausted. I had been sewing all day. Suddenly I get a text from Michael. I would've thought purposely ghosting a guy for about a week would give a pretty clear hint, but I guess not.

"Hey, want to meet for coffee tomorrow?" it read.

I rolled my eyes. I should just give him a chance, but I can't become distracted, especially not now.

Chapter Seventeen

Dylan Spencer
Friday, November 4th, 10:30 a.m.

It was about a day ago when I got that letter. I wasn't sure what to do next. Brooklyn has been in communication with the girl since. I love Brooklyn. She cares so much about people, in ways I admire. She quickly wanted to make the girl feel safe, and I adore that. She's already so busy, but she's taking time to communicate with her almost every hour. I'm not sure what the status of everything is or how quickly they'd be able to handle everything. My only job was to find them a solid lawyer, preferably not a man. Only one solid lawyer comes to mind. Her name is Jenifer J. Green. She studied at Harvard Law School. I met her once when I was at this conference that my grandfather dragged me to. She's only twenty-five, which is extremely impressive. I had a feeling her services would be extremely expensive, and I'm sure my family would wonder why I was paying for a lawyer. So in order for this to work and for my grandfather to not find out, I'd have to stay out of it. I wouldn't be able to help because I could risk him finding out and completely scaring this girl out of coming forward.

I'm sure once she comes forward, many other young girls will as well. I remember when I first came to this campus, people would whisper about him, and I'd just shrug it off, but now it makes sense, and I will not rest another second until he is behind bars.

Another issue that comes with my grandfather is his racism. He's always been that way. My mom usually received the worst parts of it. When she married my father, my grandpa wouldn't even really acknowledge her much. My nana loved my mom. She would always defend her whenever he'd say anything relentless. In a way, I believe my father is scared of him. I can't even imagine the things he's had to endure. My dad is pretty stone cold. For as long as I can remember, he has never shown an ounce of emotion. He's never cried, and I've never seen him really smile. He'd do that weak half smile, but never a genuine one. I guess that's something he learned.

I remember the very first time I brought Brooklyn home. It was Easter. I had dated Brookie for a few months, almost a year, before bringing her home. I knew how my grandfather was. When we walked into the house, we walked into the foyer, which had a marble floor and a stairway that led up high. His wife Elaine ran up and hugged Brookie. My mom gave her a hug also, as did Evie. They practically talked her head off for about an hour. Then my father came and just talked her head off about her research.

Then, when my grandfather came, he didn't even really acknowledge her. He just gave a half smile and asked where the food was. He even made a snarky comment like, "I guess you learned from your father." I'm pretty sure he had been drinking a bit and wasn't really in the right mindset, which I'm sure he is never fully sober. It amazes me still how he's able to maintain being in charge of a college and be as rich as he is. My mom still doesn't like him too much. She's been in this family longer than I've been alive. Although my dad isn't around too much, he would always defend my mom. He'd go off on Grandpa; cuss him out if he came out his mouth wrong to mom. Although that didn't stop him from saying things. Then a big argument would spark, and then dad would storm out, and I would take Evie upstairs to play so she wouldn't have to hear these things. I always wanted to protect Evie. I would do anything for her. She's so young, and she has so much joy in her. I can see it in her little, light eyes. She's a lot like my mom in that way. I never want her to lose that light.

I was lazy today. I didn't have much work to do. I sort of just laid here. I was trying to digest everything. I even texted Lucas to ask how the phone stuff was going. He said he's been working, but it's been nearly impossible to narrow down the location of the texts. He said they pinged off the phone tower near the city, so they really could be anywhere. I even tried to make sure I wouldn't get the emails, so I blocked the email account. It wasn't that easy, though; I still got emails from different accounts.

Time went by quickly. I decided to visit Mom and Evie for a bit. They've been staying in a house in New York, which is about thirty minutes from campus. I'm not sure about the house in Pennsylvania. I haven't been back there since I graduated from high school. I went to see how they were. Evie isn't feeling the best. She's had a cold for the past day or so. I walked into the house, and I was greeted by my mom.

"Hi, my sweet boy. I just saw you Tuesday, but I missed you so much," she said.

"I missed you too, mama," I said back. "There was some mail for you I believe. It's in there on the counter. I didn't open it," she said.

I nod and make my way into the kitchen. There was a big stack of mail. I shuffled through the stack for a few minutes, and I saw a package for me and an envelope. I opened the package, and it was just some headphones I had ordered the other week. The envelope just said my name and had my address on the cover. I ripped it open, and there was a letter. The letter read:

Dylan,
NEVER
BELIEVE
A
LIAR

That's all the paper read. "Never believe a liar." What did that mean? I look into the envelope, and I see another letter. It's the same letter that the girl wrote to me. It wasn't identical word for word, but some phrases were the same. But on top of the letter, "LIAR" was written in red, in big, sloppy wording. I started to panic because how would they have this letter?

After leaving home, I went into my room at my apartment to search for the letter. It's still there in my drawer, untouched. Not only does this person have close access into my life, but now they know about someone whose trauma was supposed to be kept a secret. Why did this girl's own personal trauma come up? Then it made sense. Does this person not want her to come forward? Why would they want her to suffer if their animosity is toward me? So, I decided to call Lucas to see what he'd think about this person sending me mail.

Dylan: Lucas, you there?

Lucas: Hello, Dylan. No, your phone is not ready.

Dylan: I'm calling to ask a question, man.

Lucas: What?

Dylan: Who would have access to my own personal info here? Would anyone in your office have access?

Lucas: All personal information is stored for staff and people with presidential status here. Or the interns, which is unlikely.

Dylan: Oh.

Lucas: Why? Something happened?

Dylan: Just got something weird in the mail. That's all.

Lucas: I know there's been issues in the past with leaked info. Considering you are pretty popular here, someone could've gotten paid to release your information.

Dylan: That's a thing here?

Lucas: Hell yeah, it wouldn't surprise me if that's what happened to you.

Dylan: If I give you my computer, can you trace IP addresses?

Lucas: Yes. You can bring it tomorrow. I'll be in the office until noon.

Dylan: Alright, man, thanks.

Lucas: Of course.

Chapter Eighteen

Brooklyn Reed
Friday, November 4th, 1:30 p.m.

Fridays are my easiest days. I just have Spanish writing. I never imagined taking this much Spanish in college. I like Spanish. It's hard, but I love the challenge. Most people took Spanish courses in high school, but I didn't take many Spanish classes. I just took two, and I intended on switching to French. Then, at orientation, I just switched to Spanish. It also helped me talk to Dylan's mom when I first met her. I guess I just wanted to impress her, and it's fun to talk with Dylan in Spanish. He said that growing up, his mom would only speak to them in Spanish. So they really had no choice but to learn it.

I have an exam coming up this Monday. So I decided to head to Starbucks after class. I walked in, and it was empty today. New York is beautiful, especially on gloomy days. I sat at a two-seat table by the window. I decided to order my favorite drink, which is an iced white mocha with an extra shot of espresso. I always order a *grande*. I could've gotten the venti, but that much coffee would make my head spin. I turned on my "gloomy days" playlist and hit shuffle. I open my book bag to get my Spanish book out. I go to page 207 and start practicing present subjunctives, which is a difficult concept sometimes. I studied for a good thirty or so minutes with every Peter Bradley Adams song on repeat. I opened my email to check to see if I missed any emails today. I see an email with no subject and just an image. The image is of Dylan and me, and we were sitting down in the lobby of my building. It looks as though it's a screenshot taken on a security camera. I was wondering that night why Dylan wanted to sit so far in the back of the lobby. I'm guessing to avoid the cameras. But how would this person have this picture? I was wondering if this is why Dylan has been so jumpy...Is he receiving stuff like this? I downloaded the image to my computer, and I blocked the email address. I began my assignment for Spanish, which took me over two hours.

I've been communicating with this girl for a day or so, and I've learned a lot about her in that time. I learned she's from Cuba, which is why I believe Dylan took it so seriously. His mom is from Cuba. The girl likes to spend time with her family, and she's been upset because she hasn't been able to see them. She told me she finished her statement in one night. She emailed it to me, and I read it so many times. I was nearly in tears. You can tell she has had something stolen from her.

I was able to reach out to Jenifer J. Green. Dylan said that she studied at Harvard Law School. I called her office, and they gave me her direct line, and I'm about to call now. It's currently 3:45 p.m. I walk outside to my car, and I call her number.

Jenifer: Hey, this is Jenifer speaking.
Brooklyn: Hello, my name's Brooklyn.
Jenifer: Hello, Brooklyn. What can I do for you?

Brooklyn: Well, I actually need legal representation for one of my friends who was sexually assaulted.

Jenifer: What is your friend's name?

Brooklyn: Well, I don't really know; she didn't tell me. She came forward anonymously to my boyfriend.

Jenifer: Can you tell me the name of the abuser?

Brooklyn: Marcus Spencer. He's the president of Morrid University.

Jenifer: Marcus Spencer?

Brooklyn: Do you know him?

Jenifer: Not personally; I have heard of him. Has the victim written her statement?

Brooklyn: Yes, she has.

Jenifer: Is there evidence of the abuse, physically?

Brooklyn: She also has the underwear from that night in a Ziplock bag.

Jenifer: She's a smart girl to keep that concealed. Do you know if she had a rape kit done?

Brooklyn: No, ma'am. She did not.

Jenifer: When did this assault occur?

Brooklyn: It occurred on April 28th, a year ago.

Jenifer: So it has been a bit of time since then, so a rape kit isn't necessarily going to be as accurate now. I'm willing to represent her legally.

Brooklyn: Really?

Jenifer: Yes. Although my case experience is typically with homicides, I will make an exception with this.

Brooklyn: Thank you!

Jenifer: These processes are extensive and don't offer a lot of time, so it's vital we begin now.

Brooklyn: What's first?

Jenifer: I would like to speak with the victim as soon as possible.

Brooklyn: How soon?

Jenifer: Today. My office closes at six. Although this case seems high profile, I do know that Marcus Spencer has many acquaintances in this office. I would prefer to keep this quiet. Only the people in the office I trust are involved in this case.

Brooklyn: I really appreciate that!

Jenifer: Do you think you can both meet with me today at six? My staff will most likely be gone.

Brooklyn: I can try. As for payment, I know your services are expensive, so I may have to just do a payment plan and pay monthly.

Jenifer: No worries. I can do this pro bono.

Brooklyn: Are you sure?

Jenifer: Positive. Today at six. See you then.

Brooklyn: See you then.

How am I going to be able to get her to agree to meet with a lawyer this soon? Everything is moving quickly.

I texted her, saying, "Got us one of the best lawyers in Manhattan. We have to meet her today. Are you okay with this?"

She responded almost instantly with, "Are you sure this is safe? What if he knows the people in the office?"

"The lawyer said that we can meet there around six when her office is closing, so no one will know the details of this case," I texted.

"What's the address?" she asked.

"59 W. 10th St., New York, NY, 10011."

The time went by quickly. I arrived at the firm, and to my surprise, she came. She was shorter and had black hair. She is stunning. She walks up to me.

"Let's go in," she said.

I nod my head. We walked into the building, and it's empty aside from security. At the top of the stairs in the building, there's a tall, skinny, blonde woman.

"Girls follow me," she said.

We follow her up the stairs to a room down the hall. The building was so modernized. Everything was glass, even the walls. We took a seat in a conference room with the blonde lady sitting across from us.

"I'm Jenifer, but you can call me JJ; who is who?" JJ asked.

"My name's Brooklyn," I said.

"My name is Veronica," Veronica said, hesitantly.

"Veronica, can you tell me what happened? I have to have a verbal statement," JJ said.

"I wrote everything down; can I just read that?" Veronica asked.

"Of course you can," said JJ.

Veronica explained what happened.

"I will stop at nothing to make sure he is prosecuted, Veronica. You can trust me. I will do my best to get you justice," said JJ.

"Thank you, but how do we even do this?" Veronica asks.

"That's why this is going to be tricky. The first step now is to get the evidence and everything processed. We will verify that it's his semen on the underwear, and after that, we can subpoena him to court. I'll have my coworkers handle the paperwork. We will keep your identity sealed. He will not know who is pressing charges until we are in the courtroom. How does that sound?" JJ explained.

"It actually sounds really good. Thank you. Any idea on how long this will take?" Veronica asked.

"There's no specific timeline, but it can take weeks, even months. Once the evidence is processed this week, court can happen the week after. If evidence takes longer, then it will take longer for court, but since you have the underwear sealed, there's a chance they can quickly process it. Those will be used in court," JJ explained.

"I'm so nervous. I haven't been able to have closure. I've felt so stuck," Veronica said.

"Well, now, you have a team behind you fighting for justice," I said.

"Brooklyn is right. I'm more than qualified to handle this case. I will work on your paperwork this weekend. We will keep this under wraps. Please get the underwear to me today; that gives them the weekend to analyze it," JJ stated.

"So, as far as testifying, who would testify?" Veronica asked.

"Well, you would tell the jury what happened. Brooklyn would technically be called to the stand since she knows the specifics of the incident. The medical examiner would speak on the underwear," JJ explained.

"Would Dylan have to speak?" I asked.

"No. Dylan would not speak simply because he's related to the defendant. He must stay as far away as he can from this case because he could risk the confidence of it," JJ explained.

"What do I do now?" Veronica asked.

"You let me handle it. I will do everything in my power to help you. Your body is your temple; it's not supposed to be violated, and when it is, we do everything we can to make sure the person who does it is put away. I've also heard about the man. He makes many women uncomfortable and should not be in a position of power over anyone," JJ said.

"We will get you justice, Veronica; as long as it takes, we will do this. I will be by your side the entire way. and I will not leave your side," I explained.

I was sad that I couldn't tell Dylan anything. But I understand it's in Veronica's best interest. It feels weird knowing her name now. I always thought of her as a mystery, as if not knowing her name would bring ease. She looks exactly how I sort of pictured she would. She also has a strong Cuban accent, and she's sort of a shy speaker. When she talks, she doesn't really maintain eye contact at all. She said she does all her classes online now to avoid having to ever see him, and she only went to her class in person that day to give Dylan the letter. I hate that she has to go through this. I'm sure once Marcus finds out what is happening, he's going to lawyer up immediately. I'm guessing that's why this has to be kept quiet for as long as possible. I hate that I had to miss Dylan's game, but he said he understood.

Chapter Nineteen

Reese Woods
Monday, November 7th, 10:45 a.m.

Mariah and I have been busy all weekend. We've been putting together everything for this business. We ordered fabrics, sketch pads, and everything. Mariah even ordered this sewing machine that can sew numerous things in such a short period of time. Needless to say, it's going to take us a while to get things in order. I woke up around a decent time this morning. I was sketching and making sure I had all my things ready for school this week. I hadn't really seen Brooklyn or Dylan at all this weekend. I guess they were off just doing their own thing. It's been a boring weekend.

I decided I'd get ready for class, so I turned on the TV. I usually watch tv while I get ready because it's just background noise. The news came on this morning, so it wasn't really of interest to me until I heard, "Morrid University President Potentially Facing Sexual Assault Charges," said the news reporter. The president of the university is Dylan's grandfather. I wonder if Dylan has heard of the accusation. If so, he sure as hell didn't tell me. This could potentially be really bad for him if his family is facing heat. The school doesn't like bad attention at all, especially not negative press like this. When the person in charge of our school is facing charges, there's no telling how badly things can escalate here.

"A source in the Manhattan Law Firm has come forward, stating that a young woman is pursuing legal action regarding the assault she faced from the university president. While there hasn't been any clarification from the president, the school could potentially be under fire along with him. More details about this will be coming soon once there is more to come to light," said the news reporter.

Chapter Twenty

Mariah Parker
Monday, November 7th, 10:45 a.m.

It's been a weird morning here on campus. Everyone's talking about the thing with Dylan's grandpa. This could explain why Dylan was acting weird, aside from the stalkerish person after him. Stuff like this doesn't really happen on our campus. At least not that I know of. Now I'm wondering if Brooklyn knew about this. Is this why he wanted to talk to her alone? Looks like I'm going to have to ask Dylan. He can't deny it now.

> Mariah: Dylan?
> Dylan: Hey.
> Mariah: Dylan, what is going on?
> Dylan: A lot.
> Mariah: Did you know about this stuff?
> Dylan: Yeah, I did. It wasn't supposed to get out though.
> Mariah: Then how did it get out?
> Dylan: I don't know, but this is bad. He's gonna be furious.

Mariah: He didn't know about it?

Dylan: No, he didn't. He wasn't supposed to find out yet.

Mariah: Dylan, did you help this happen?

Dylan: Mariah. Why would I help this story get out?

Mariah: No, I mean, did you help this legal stuff get started?

Dylan: No, Mariah, I didn't know the details.

Mariah: But you knew enough.

Dylan: Who's side are you on?

Mariah: Dylan, I'm on your side. Just confused why you didn't tell your friends.

Dylan: It wasn't my business to tell Mariah. I didn't even know about it. Not the details.

Mariah: But you knew about her?

Dylan: Yes, I did. I just couldn't know the details of the legal stuff because I'm related to him.

Mariah: Oh, that makes sense. What is your family going to do? This is about to be publicized everywhere. Isn't the game against Brown this Friday?

Dylan: Yeah, they'll probably cancel it. This is bad press for the school.

Mariah: You didn't come today, right?

Dylan: Nah, I'm in my room. Didn't want to hear what people had to say.

Mariah: Do you think Brooklyn came?

Dylan: Yeah, she had a Spanish exam. She said she was gonna leave after.

Mariah: Imagine the stares she's gonna get because she dates you.

Dylan: Yeah, I feel bad. I hate that she's gonna have to deal with this.

Mariah: Yeah, same. I'm in the cafe; I came in here for breakfast. Everyone's talking about it. I wish I could help.

Dylan: Just stick by her side today.

Mariah: I'll try my best.

Dylan: Mariah, keep me updated.

Mariah: I will. Sorry, this is happening.

Dylan: It's fine. It'll be okay. Take care of my girl.

Mariah: I will. I promise.

Chapter Twenty-One

Dylan Spencer
Monday, November 7th, 11:00 a.m.

This was not supposed to happen at all. It was supposed to be a secret. Someone leaked this information…But who would do this? Who would have access to this information? A part of me feels like this was my fault. I dropped Brooklyn off at the firm. What if someone followed us there? Snuck in and ruined this whole thing. My grandpa has time to plan this whole thing out and come up with his lies. Now my mom is calling me…

Dylan: Hey, Mom.

Alicia: Dylan, have you seen the news?

Dylan: Yeah.

Alicia: What is this all about, Dylan?

Dylan: I guess Marcus is facing charges.

Alicia: Your father was swarmed by the press coming into the house.

Dylan: The news crew is at the house?

Alicia: Yes, they won't leave. I've had to keep Evie upstairs with me.

Dylan: I'm coming to the house.

Alicia: Dylan, are you sure that's a good idea?

Dylan: I'm already walking to my car.

Alicia: Be safe. See you soon.

Before I knew it, I had my keys in my hand, and I was cranking my car up. The ride home was short, and my thoughts were everywhere. I was driving so fast, I'm sure I broke a law or something. My head is spinning. I don't understand why the press is harassing us and not the monster of this story. I pulled up to the house, and there's a news truck, hundreds of people with cameras, and there's plenty of news reporters everywhere.

I get out of my car, and at this point, I'm livid. I walk toward the door, and I'm stopped by a lady slowing me down, saying, "Dylan Spencer, what do you think of the allegations against your grandfather? Do you believe he's a sexual predator?" she said.

Without thinking, I responded, "How about instead of asking me about him, you ask him why he's being accused of sexual assault in the first place?" I walked up the porch and slammed the door. Inside, my dad is on the phone, to which he hangs up as soon as I enter.

"Dylan, is it still crazy out there?" he asked.

"There are people everywhere," I said.

"Do you know anything about these allegations, Dylan?" Dad asked.

"I know enough." I sighed.

"Do you believe the allegations?" he asked.

"Dad, do you?" I asked back.

"I know my father, but I also know the way he talks about women. I'll always believe the woman, which is why I asked you," he said.

"Of course, I believe her dad. What is going to happen?" I asked.

"Well your grandfather lawyered up the second the source came forward. He doesn't understand the depth of the situation or how his actions are going to finally catch up with him. Some of the things he's done haven't even come out yet," Dad explained.

"Things like what, Dad?" I asked.

"Your grandfather's no award-winning citizen, Dylan. He's been accused of money laundering too. That was when I was a teenager though. I'm not sure what the status is with that, but I remember it," Dad said.

"Why have you stayed by his side all this time?" I asked.

"I don't want to. I want nothing more than to cut him out of our lives, Dyl. I know what he's capable of. You see the way he treats your mother and Evie. He simply doesn't like the fact that they look different than we do. I don't want Evie to grow up around that. I just don't know how to," Dad explained.

"I understand that. Hopefully he gets locked up for this though," I said.

"I sure hope so. Go upstairs with mom and Evie to check on them. I'm on the phone with security trying to get rid of these people outside the house," Dad said.

I go up to check on Mom and Evie. Evie is just sitting on the floor playing with her barbies, and my mom is sitting on her bed watching TV.

"Hey, Dyl Dyl," sings Evie as she runs up to hug me.

"I see you're feeling better, Evie," I said.

"Her cough is gone, but her nose is still a bit stuffy," Mom said.

I take a seat on Evie's bed, relax here for a few minutes, and talk to Mom about school. She asks how Brooklyn's doing and smiles as I tell her all about Brooklyn. I tell her how Brooklyn is doing really well with her classes and how our relationship is really healthy. I think she can tell how serious I am about Brooklyn. Yeah, I had been in other relationships, but I had never really settled down or saw a future with any of the girls. So, I usually ended things before they got too attached.

Downstairs, we hear a bang on the door. It's loud enough that it startles me. I run downstairs, and I look at my dad in his office on the phone. I open the door, and there's my grandfather. He walks into the house and shoves me up against the wall by my neck.

"How could you say that on the news? You're ruining my image," he argued.

"You're ruining your image all on your own," I struggled to say back. I try to shove him off, but I can't. I feel powerless. Just like when I was a scrawny kid.

My dad runs out and pushes him off me. "Get your hands off him!" my dad shouted.

"Tell him to keep his damn mouth shut," my grandpa said as he stormed out of the house, slamming the door behind him.

I catch my breath. I look over at my dad; he sighs. I walked into the living room to see the news, and there I was. "Morrid President is facing allegations. Here is what his grandson has to say," the caption read. I couldn't believe he came all the way to our house to shuffle me up. I guess I should've just kept my mouth shut, but I was irritated, so I just responded back to the reporter without even thinking. I wish the cameras were rolling on him when he did that. So they could capture how violent he was sometimes. My phone rings, and it's Reese.

Reese: Dylan, what the hell is happening?

Dylan: A lot. I can't even explain it all.

Reese: Did you know about the allegations?

Dylan: Yeah. I wasn't supposed to say any-thing. Sorry, I didn't tell you.

Reese: I understand. I saw you on the news.

Dylan: Should've seen my grandpa's reaction.

Reese: Did he put his hands on you?

Dylan: Yeah, he came to the house, grabbed me by the neck, and shoved me to the wall.

Reese: And this is the guy they're letting be our president on campus?

Dylan: Yeah, it's crazy.

Reese: Sorry to hear that, Dylan.

Dylan: It's cool. I'm used to it.

Reese: How did you get him off you?

Dylan: Dad pushed him off.

Reese: Really?

Dylan: Yeah. He was angry.

Reese: I don't blame him. His dad putting his hands on his kid had to have bothered him.

Dylan: Yeah, I guess.

Reese: Does he know how physical your grandpa was with you growing up?

Dylan: Yeah, he does. The bruises on me were self-explanatory. And he stopped sending me over there.

Reese: Wow, Dyl, sorry about that.

Everyone was always sorry. No one knew how to handle it. My dad doesn't even acknowledge him too much; he almost seems shaken up around him, which begged the question. Was my dad abused too? Now I want to know.

"Dad, can I talk to you?" I asked, walking into his office.

"What's up, Dylan?" he responded.

"Did grandpa ever put his hands on you growing up?" I asked hesitantly.

"Why'd you ask?" he questioned.

"Because of the bruises he would leave on me. Figured he may have done that to you too," I say.

"Your grandfather made my life hell. He hated every move I made. Imagine his anger with me when I brought home a Cuban woman who I told him I wanted to marry," he explains.

"How did that go?" I asked even though I already knew the answer.

"He was mad. He didn't understand why I loved her. I was in high school, so I didn't know why he was so mad. I didn't understand where his hatred had stemmed from," Dad says.

"Did he say anything to you about when I brought Brooke home?" I asked curiously.

"He said, 'like father, like son,'" Dad said.

"How did you feel about it?" I asked.

"Well, I never understood the whole race thing anyway. I mean, you see your mother; she's not white. Her skin color didn't affect how much I loved her. That stuff doesn't matter; it's just the way he is, I guess," he explained.

I guess he had a point. In this world, everyone is so focused on skin color that it affects who a person falls in love with. Now, I feel powerless. The whole point of keeping this a secret was to allow everything to be figured out without the press's input. Now, I'm more than sure my grandfather has lawyered up. Considering he's a lawyer himself, this case is going to be a piece of cake for him, which isn't fair. I never understood how there can be so much evidence, and they just let these monsters walk free.

Since my dad told me about the money laundering, I can't help but wonder how that could affect this case. Is there a way this could help the girl? That would prove how much of a liar he is; at least it would get him some jail time. I couldn't help but ask the question of how I would possibly be able to prove that. The only way that stuff is done is with either a private investigator or the government doing some digging. Considering how wealthy my grandfather is, there is no telling how much money he's laundered. Now that I have some money saved, I wonder if I should hire a private investigator to dig into this so I wouldn't have to do it on my own.

After a bit of digging, I was able to narrow it down. I found a PI who charges about $6,500, which is expensive, but I expected it considering this isn't an easy task, especially money laundering itself. My grandfather is a smart man, despite everything. I'm sure he's able to cover his tracks very well, so I had to find a PI who was good at their job. I found a guy named Detective Clark. I asked him to meet me to talk. He asked if we could meet today, which was way sooner than I thought. I figured he'd want more time to discuss or know more of the details. He's requesting the money upfront, which seems pretty sketchy, but maybe he's thinking I'll back out and not give him his money.

The next thing I had to do was run to the ATM to take out $6,500. PI's usually have to be paid in cash rather than by card. I met Detective Clark at a diner called "Lewis's Diner." I know the owner pretty well; he's an older guy, but nice. The diner is pretty small and older, but Lewis makes some great waffles and eggs. I find a booth at the back of the diner a little bit isolated. I take a seat, and I keep the envelope in my hoodie pocket. Exactly six thousand and five hundred dollars in cash.

Not only was this decision to get a PI insanely last minute and impulsive, but I'm sure my parents are gonna ask why I withdrew this much money out of the bank all of a sudden. I figured I'd have to come up with a big lie or an excuse that sounds half ass enough for them not to question me any further about it. I wasn't really the best liar at all. I tend to smile or laugh and get nervous. It reminds me of how nervous I got on my first date with Brooklyn.

About two years ago, I had been texting and talking to Brooklyn for a few weeks. We both didn't really see it going anywhere, I don't think. Then, out of nowhere, I just got the courage to ask her out on a date. It took everything in me not to back out of it. I had talked to her for a while, but she still made me so nervous. It was around 7:25 p.m. when I picked her up from her dorm. She looked stunning. She was wearing an all-black romper thing that girls wear. It was so subtle, but so beautiful on her. She was wearing these black slip-on heels that made her a little bit taller. She got into the passenger seat, put her seat belt on, and just smiled at me. She didn't say much, but I could tell she was nervous too. Then, on the radio, the song "Can't Help Falling in Love" by Elvis Presley started to play. At first, she just smiled when it started, then she started to shift side to side slowly, then she started to hum. I could hear the quiet humming, so I started to hum along with her. She looked at me and smiled. Her brown eyes started to sparkle; I swear. I hadn't known a girl to like Elvis as much as Brooklyn seemed to.

When the song was over, I asked her if she liked Elvis, and she laughed and said, "Well, I more than like him; love is the word." Since that night, that song has been our song. When we go to most places, we play that song, we hold hands, and sing to it.

The rest of that night was perfect. I took her to this fancy restaurant. At the time, I just assumed Brooklyn came from money because of how put together she was and how she dressed. That night she told me she had never been to a place that nice, and I asked her why not. She then said that growing up, her mom just cooked; she'd watch her cook, and after time, it just became routine. I smiled because I could relate to that. My mom used to cook her Cuban recipes, and I loved each and every one.

At dinner, Brooklyn ordered salmon and garlic-seasoned broccoli, which was funny because it was a steakhouse. That night, I learned she really didn't like steak or any meat. She told me she hated hot dogs, hamburgers, fried chicken, and even steak. Basically, all the super good foods she didn't like. She said instead that she preferred to eat seafood or even vegetables. I guess the seafood part was because she grew up by the beach. On the other hand, I'm not too fond of vegetables. My mom used to have to bribe me with toys for me to eat them as a child, and I still don't really like veggies.

Dinner with Brooklyn was perfect, and I learned a lot about her that night. After dinner we drove past the Brooklyn Bridge. Which is ironic, right? She laughed when we got there because of the irony of it all. I told her to notice how beautiful it was at night and how much her beauty reminded me of the way the city lights up at night. When you look at the surroundings, you see all the buildings and colorful lights that illuminated the city. Brooklyn was that light in a way. I really hadn't met anyone quite like her, and I wasn't about to let her slip through my hands, so that night I asked her if she wanted to be my girlfriend. I could tell she was hesitant to say yes, but she did say yes. I felt a sense of relief when I heard her say that three-letter word. I imagined she'd say something else, like no or hell no. I know I wasn't at all like Brooklyn pictured me to be. I practically clung to her every word. I was a complete hopeless romantic guy when it came to her in ways I had never truly been before. I still get nervous when I see her, as if it were that night all over again.

After twenty minutes of waiting, the PI finally showed up. He was shorter than me and a bit chubby, not fat, but you could say he had some weight. He was pale, had black hair, and a goatee. He took his seat across from me and asked what I needed from him.

"I need you to find evidence of money laundering for a man named Marcus Spencer," I said.

"Well, I knew you looked familiar; you must be Dylan Spencer. That's your grandfather," Detective Clark said.

"Yes, he is. I need this information immediately," I said firmly.

"Woah, there, son, where's the money?" he asked.

"Before I give you this money, I expect updates from you often," I demanded.

"How often? This should take me a few days," he said.

"Doesn't matter how often, as long as you let me know whenever you find information," I said.

"Now where exactly should I look?" he asked.

"Bank accounts and statements. Since he's rich, he uses private banking," I explained.

"Money," he said as he reached his hand out.

I handed him the money, and he looked at me and said, "I'll try my best, and I will keep you updated." He gets up and walks out.

I guess that was that. Now I just wait... This made me wonder. Did the person who sent me that letter with the words "Liar" on it release this information?

Chapter Twenty-Two

Brooklyn Reed
Monday, November 7th, 2:45 p.m.

The Spanish exam almost killed me. The exam was over two hours. I was almost done, and suddenly my brain just caved in. I kept my calm, but it was nearly impossible to get to the end of that exam. I don't know what made me take Spanish writing. As I packed up my bookbag, I could hear the whispers of everyone. I check my phone, and I have over twenty notifications from Dylan, Mariah, and Reese. I walked out of the classroom, and there were people in the halls looking around and whispering. I headed to an empty classroom and closed the door. I called Dylan immediately.

Brooklyn: Hey, Dylan, what's going on here? Everyone's being super weird. Looking and whispering like we're still in high school.

Dylan: Are you alone now?

Brooklyn: Yes, why?

Dylan: The news leaked about the sexual assault allegations.

Brooklyn: What? How?

Dylan: I'm not sure, but a source came forward. They don't know her name, but it's only a matter of time before they know her identity.

Brooklyn: I don't know how this happened. We just went to JJ Friday.

Dylan: It wasn't JJ who leaked it; it was someone in her office.

Brooklyn: But when we went there, we were the only ones there in the room.

Dylan: What about in the halls? Was there anyone?

Brooklyn: I suppose there may have been some people in their offices still, but how would they have heard?

Dylan: There's no telling, but my grandfather has lawyered up. He's going to try his hardest to fight this.

Brooklyn: I don't understand. What exactly does the press know?

Dylan: They know that he's being accused of sexual assault. They said an inside source came forward.

Brooklyn: An inside source?

Dylan: I'm pretty sure my grandfather has some influence there since he was a lawyer and all lawyers talk.

Brooklyn: Do you think he may have friends at the firm?

Dylan: Most likely.

Brooklyn: This is bad, Dylan. Veronica is already nervous about coming forward. How is this gonna make her feel?

Dylan: She may be even more worried now, but promise me, you will make sure she isn't alone in this.

Brooklyn: I promise, Dylan.

Dylan: I love you, okay? The press may try to get a statement from you since we are together, but please don't say anything. I already did.

Brooklyn: I love you too, Dylan. What did you say to the press?

Dylan: Basically, not denying the accusations. My grandfather was pissed; he even shuffled me up a bit.

Brooklyn: Are you okay?

Dylan: Yeah, I'm fine.

Brooklyn: Are you sure?

Dylan: I promise.

Knowing that this has officially made headlines has me concerned. What if Veronica feels silenced? What if she calls this whole case off? I needed to text and check on her.

12:45 p.m.

Brooklyn: Veronica, checking in to see how you are.

Veronica: I'm okay. It's weird to see this on TV.

Brooklyn: Do you still want to go through with this?

Veronica: Yeah, I think so. I'm just glad no one knows my identity.

Brooklyn: Yeah, I'm glad that didn't get out.

Veronica: Can you talk to JJ? See if she knows anything.

Brooklyn: Yeah, I'll call her now.

Veronica: Thanks. Talk to you soon.

Before I called JJ, I took a second to think. I couldn't help but feel emotional. Something really tragic happened here, and the media is focused on the wrong things. Not only does this glorify Marcus Spencer, but it is silencing victims everywhere to see how an accuser is being sympathized by the media. To my surprise, JJ is calling me.

JJ: Hey, Brooklyn, I have an update!

Brooklyn: Hey, JJ; tell me.

JJ: Forensics was able to collect DNA from the underwear Veronica turned in, matching Marcus Spencer. Since this evidence was collected, authorities were notified, and a warrant is out for his arrest. Things are picking up quicker than anticipated now.

Brooklyn: Wow, that happened quickly. Forensics was able to do that within two days of receiving it?

JJ: Yes, initially I believed it would have taken longer considering the semen has been present for about a year. Dry secretions on clothing are able to remain stable and collectible. So forensics worked on that over the weekend, and they were able to not only identify the presence of semen belonging to Marcus Spencer but also find traces of blood, which indicates assault from penetration.

Brooklyn: What's next?

JJ: After being taken into custody, they will collect a statement from him. A court date will be set in place. This part does require him to learn the plaintiff's name, unfortunately.

Brooklyn: So Veronica won't be anonymous anymore?

JJ: No, but I can assure you she will be safe. Marcus will be in custody, and we can have a police officer with her at all times. A female officer.

Brooklyn: So how can we keep this out of the media?

JJ: I can encourage them not to leak, but, unfortunately, he has friends everywhere that want nothing more than for him to be a free man. They may try to expose her name to the press. Veronica has to be prepared for this.

Brooklyn: Gosh, this sounds awful. What does she have to do next?

JJ: Nothing yet. I will stay in the loop on everything, and I will be able to get his statement as well.

Brooklyn: Is there anything I should do?

JJ: Be there for her, Brooklyn. This process is going to be exhausting, and she's going to feel like she is reliving this trauma. She needs a friend.

Brooklyn: I will be. Thank you so much for your help.

JJ: Of course. Call me if you need anything. Pass this information along to Veronica, and I'll see if I can get more information.

Brooklyn: Sounds good!

Chapter Twenty-Three

Reese Woods
Tuesday, November 8th, 6:30 p.m.

Everything has been hectic since the information got out about Dylan's grandfather. Dylan is on edge. I heard him pacing all night in his room. Meanwhile, I've been sketching like crazy. Ideas have just been coming to me lately; I've felt so inspired. Mariah and I have been hanging out a good bit. We've been working on logos for our business. I was thinking of those moon outlines that's like half sun and half-moon based off Mariah and my zodiac signs, but I'm not sure how that'd correlate to everything. We also decided on a business name. We're thinking of M&R Fashion', something simple like that. Today Mariah's flying home, and she won't be back till Saturday. It's her grandparents' fortieth anniversary, I think, and they're having a nice gala. I never understood how someone could stay in love for like forty-something years. It makes me sort of jealous. Imagine someone loving you unconditionally till you're really old. Mariah's supposed to say a poem at the anniversary thing. It goes like this:

Without love, how can we fully grow?

Without trust, how do we know true love?

Love is patient

Love is kind

Love is resourceful

Love is not easy

Love is timeless

So why do we fear love?

Love is vulnerable, love can be soulful, and love should not bring hurt.

Love brings us to find things in ourselves we never saw before.

Love requires us to open the door to where we can really begin to soar.

Who are we without love?

Love is what is hidden in store for us, so do not fear love.

Love is grace.

Mariah's really good at forming words together. A part of me feels like she's scared to love. Like maybe she'll love someone more than they love her. Mariah's pretty much a brick wall when it comes to emotional relationship stuff. She never really talks about that stuff. A part of me thinks she does like Michael. She's just scared to pursue it. Whenever she talks about love, it seems like such a burden, like it's on some timeline. It's just that her own personal opinions on love are so strong, and yet whenever she's giving advice, it's good advice. She just sounds like a girl whose heart has been broken way too many times.

Chapter Twenty-Four

Mariah Parker
Wednesday, November 9th, 10:30 a.m.

It feels weird being back in Boston. The penthouse hasn't changed at all. It's the same black-and-white interior. When you walk in, there's the white spiral staircase and the glass walls that allow for a view of the city. I can tell Mom and Dad don't really spend much time at home. Everything looks untouched and unlived in. My room is the best room here; it actually has some depth to it. I have my old sketches scattered on my desk, and my fabric is right on here with them. It brings me back to my senior year. It felt like fashion was my escape and my chance to be good at something. I'd get home all upset about my day, and that's when my ideas would be the best. I remember I practically designed a whole winter fashion line during my winter break. My family and I were supposed to go to Cancun, but we couldn't because Dad had to work and my mom didn't want to go without him. I was furious, but it gave me time to just sketch. Sometimes I just feel so stuck. I really want to make something of myself, but it feels like I'm making no progress. I'm good at the fashion thing, but I need more than that.

Chapter Twenty-Five

Dylan Spencer
Thursday, November 10th, 8:00 a.m.

Practice this morning wasn't the best. My head just wasn't into it, I guess. Coach pulled me aside before and wanted to know if I was feeling okay with the stuff going on. My grandfather was arrested last night at 7:00 p.m. The police showed up at his house and arrested him for the sexual assault charges. The news crew was already there, and they had the whole arrest on film. The officer said, "You have the right to remain silent. Anything you say or do can and will be used against you in a court of law," or something like that. It was sort of entertaining, but I can only imagine how this whole case is going to turn out. The most awful thing about it was that my grandfather didn't even deny anything; he just let them arrest him. I guess I was expecting him to resist a bit, but I guess he figured there was nothing he could do.

My parents cut off all contact with him. I guess that allegation was their breaking point with him. It makes me feel good to know that my family takes this stuff seriously. I felt so stuck with this whole thing. I had to remove myself from the whole case because I could've compromised it all. I'm guessing it's probably for the best. Everything has been on my mind all week. I just get so angry thinking about it. The fact that I'm related to someone who could do something like this hurts. I guess what sucks the most is knowing Veronica could see my grandpa when she looks at me. I'm even more surprised at how quickly this case has taken off. Jenifer has worked tirelessly to make sure my grandfather doesn't get away with this. I don't even feel like I should call him my grandfather; his name is Marcus. He's nothing to me.

After practice I went back to the suite to shower and wash up before I started my literature homework. When I got out of the shower, I had a missed call from Lucas. I called him back after I got dressed in some sweats.

Lucas: Dylan? Are you there?

Dylan: Yeah, man, sorry, I just got out of the shower. What's up?

Lucas: I found some information, some of which can be useful.

Dylan: Okay, what is it?

Lucas: Apparently there was a breach in the student database a few weeks ago.

Dylan: What does that mean?

Lucas: It means someone was able to hack into the database and access student files.

Dylan: Files like what?

Lucas: Student financial records, home addresses. Things I don't even have access to.

Dylan: I did receive a package at my home address. Is my home address listed in the database?

Lucas: I'm not sure, Dylan. I don't have access to those files. I'd have to dig for it.

Dylan: I need you to check. I don't think that my home address is listed there; I believe my suite address is.

Lucas: Is that something I have to do urgently?

Dylan: Yes, Lucas. This person found out my family's address another way.

Lucas: Okay. On it now; stay on the phone; it'll only take me a second.

Dylan: Thanks for doing this.

Lucas: It's no problem, really. I see here your address listed has been removed.

Dylan: Does it say when?

Lucas: In the place of the address, it just says "Spiel Weiter."

Dylan: What does that mean?

Lucas: It means "continue to play" or "game on" in German.

Dylan: Hmm…

Lucas: You never brought your computer by.

Dylan: Yeah, I know. I just blocked the emails.

Lucas: Are you still there?

Dylan: Yeah, man, give me a second; I'll call you back.

My address was once there, and now it's replaced with the words in German. That could mean a number of things. I remember getting the letter that said, "Never believe a liar" and then the "liar." Could this message be a response to the arrest of Marcus? Wait a minute…It's in German. How was

I expected to ever see that message? How did they know that Lucas knew German?

> Dylan: Hey, man, do you take German?
>
> Lucas: Yeah, I've been taking it since high school.
>
> Dylan: Does anyone know you're helping me?
>
> Lucas: No. I have not told anyone.
>
> Dylan: Okay, call if you get any more updates.
>
> Lucas: Sounds good.

No matter what I do, this person is always one step ahead of me. I have so many questions, like, how did they know I'd ask Lucas to check the database? How did they know he spoke German? But most importantly, what does "continue to play" mean? Why are they so determined to see my grandfather as innocent?

Chapter Twenty-Six

Brooklyn Reed
Thursday, November 10th, 12:30 p.m.

I invited Veronica to lunch with me today at a small, discrete place in the city. It's a place called Francia's. It's basically French food. I had never been here before. I just wanted to pick a small place, sort of away from the school. I'm sure she feels bad about this whole thing getting out. I was hesitant to ask her to meet because I didn't want to scare her off about this stuff. I just want to hear how she's feeling and her thoughts on the media coverage of the case. I understand how difficult this stuff is, especially when it's broadcast to the nation.

"Thank you for meeting me today. How are you feeling?" I asked her.

"Could be better. I feel like everywhere I turn, I see him," Veronica said, opening the menu.

"I'm sure it's so hard to see. Tell me more," I said.

"It feels like social media and stuff are leaning towards his side. I mean, what's going to happen when they find out it's me who's pursuing this case? Imagine how much they're gonna tear me apart," she explains.

"I know, it sucks. It feels like the women in these cases are never listened to. Something has to change." I sighed.

"What makes you so passionate about this? Is it that friend you told me about? If you don't mind me asking," she said.

"Well yes. It's about my friend Mackenzie," I answered.

"What happened?" Veronica asked.

"We grew up together. We did competitive gymnastics together since we were six. She was assaulted by one of our coaches, Coach Terry. I still remember everything that happened; well, what she told me. He was our floor coach. It was one weekend when we were fifteen, and we all had private lessons with him to learn our new floor routines for regionals. If we qualified for regionals, they wanted us to do a new floor routine with the same music but harder skills and routine. My practice was at 9:00 a.m., and hers was at 11:00 a.m. She told me the details of what happened and how he started touching her in places she didn't want. Then it escalated to more. She was scared to come forward about it. I was the first person she told until eventually our moms came forward and went to the head coach about everything. A big trial happened, and past gymnasts from our gym came forward, saying he did this to them. The scariest thing was how much we all looked up to him, and we had known him since we were kids. He abused that trust. Stuff like that on its own just makes me upset," I explained sincerely.

"What do you want to do with your life?" Veronica asked.

"Well, I want to be a doctor, I guess," I answered unsurely.

"That doesn't sound like the answer of someone who wants to be a doctor. If you're passionate about helping people and things like that, why don't you be a lawyer? One that advocates for victims and cares enough about them to make sure there's a fair trial," she said, closing the menu.

"I don't know if I'd be good at that," I responded back.

"You're really good at it. I see how you are with me. If it wasn't for JJ, I would've wanted you to represent me," she said with a smile.

"Really?" I asked.

"Absolutely. I see how much passion you have. Those are the people we need in this world to be lawyers. People who care and want the justice system to be fixed not only for sexual and domestic assaults but also for racial injustices also. I've been here in America for about two years, and they still won't grant me citizenship. If I go back to Cuba, I'm stuck there," she says.

"Well, I'll think about that. I really want to help people," I said.

This is true. I really listened to what Veronica said. What she said made so much sense to me; it all just clicked, I guess. So, I wanted to call Dylan when I left the restaurant.

Dylan: Hey, Brookie, what's up?

Brooklyn: Just thinking of you. I had a long talk with Veronica about everything.

Dylan: How'd that go? Is she doing okay?

Brooklyn: She's handling all this so well. She's so strong.

Dylan: I'm glad to hear she's doing good.

Brooklyn: Dyl?

Dylan: Yeah?

Brooklyn: Could you see me doing something with the law?

Dylan: After this whole thing, I would say yes. You're doing a great job. I can tell you care.

We need more lawyers like this. Less like my grandfather.

Brooklyn: I agree. Thanks for that.

Dylan: Of course, beautiful. I'm headed to get something to eat. Talk to you in a bit?

Brooklyn: Yeah. Be safe. Love you.

Dylan: Love you more.

Chapter Twenty-Seven

Veronica Álvarez—Her perspective

Growing up, it was always family first. Family was everything; family was to be valued. I've always been attached to the hip with my family. My older sister, Brianna, is my hero. She's gone through more than I could even imagine. She was sixteen when she got pregnant by the guy she thought she loved. I guess everything happens for a reason, and his true character was brought to light when he heard the news of her pregnancy. He didn't want anything to do with her and left her that same day. This hit Brianna hard. I guess, in a way, it reminded her of her father. She and I have different dads. I was young when I learned about that. Her dad chose drugs and women over his child. It's unfortunate that stuff happens. I guess I got lucky with my dad; he's been there every step of the way. He and my mom always kept me on a tight lease as a child.

I was pretty much oblivious to the dangers around me most of the time. I guess that's why my parents were hesitant to send me to the US. I didn't know much English and only really spoke Spanish. I guess what happened to me is every parent's nightmare. To have their child violated and assaulted in the way I was. Initially, I hadn't really heard much about Morrid University here in Cuba. I knew before applying to colleges that I wanted to study law. Morrid University didn't have much of a law program, but they offered pretty good internships. Sure enough, weeks went by, and I decided to apply there without even telling my parents. I used my money I was saving for a while to pay the application fee. A few months went by, and I got accepted. I was so excited, I figured it was meant to be. So I proudly told my parents, and they weren't initially the happiest about it. They practically refused to acknowledge it at first and just went silent for a few minutes. After a while, they opened up their minds to the idea. I think what made them allow me to go is the fact they never got to go to college, and they wanted me to be able to.

The next thing I knew, I was off to New York City that August. It felt unreal to be able to go to a school like Morrid. All the students there were extremely rich. Their parents could pay off their whole tuition in one payment. My parents, on the other hand, had a payment plan and paid monthly. It wasn't easy for them, and it still isn't. Morrid doesn't give many scholarships at all. Mostly rich people come here, athletes, and science people. I wasn't really interested in science, so that scholarship wasn't even an option. Adjusting here was extremely hard. I didn't really know the language, so I had to have my lectures recorded and translated via the tech center. I eventually started to grasp the language better, but it was not easy. So when I got the internship, I was so happy. I figured I wouldn't have gotten it.

The first day at the office was intimidating. The internship took place in the president's building. It's this tall building on campus, located pretty far away from the dorms. When I went into the building, I was in complete admiration. Everything in there seemed so ahead of its time. Everything was technology based and modernized. Almost everything was made out of glass and looked so expensive. I didn't fit in here. Everyone was wearing Ralph Lauren and Chanel. I felt so out of place. I came in with my all-black dress. It was pretty tight, but it was the only business casual outfit I had in my closet. I paired it with my black heels and my fake pearls. I walked into President Spencer's office. It was spacious. He had a huge window with a view of the city. A sitting area with a black leather couch and a glass table. His desk was pretty big and organized. Everything was organized; nothing was out of place. He saw me walk in and didn't lose eye contact at all.

When I entered, he said, "You must be Veronica Álvarez."

I nodded, and he motioned for me to take a seat across from him. I sat down and just looked around. I remember him asking me about my upbringing and telling me how he enjoyed reading my application for the internship. He said he could tell I was going to be a good asset to his staff, and he looked forward to working with me. I worked my ass off for weeks, and eventually things changed.

One day I started to feel uncomfortable. Marcus had always been flirty. He was flirty with everyone in the office, so I just assumed that's just how he was. He would say things about my appearance, more specifically what I was wearing. The attire was always business casual. So that meant a dress or a skirt. He would say provocative things, sexual things. Things I've tried to forget. I thought if I said something about it, I'd lose my internship and the stipend that came along with it. I didn't want that to happen. He was the closest thing to a mentor in the law field. My job consisted of pretty much busy work: printing things, charting for the finances, documenting disciplinary papers, and organizing the scholarship files. There wasn't much law stuff going on, but that wasn't the point of the internship. I just thought he'd be able to be an important person for a recommendation letter, and I thought if I showed him how hardworking I was, he'd write a good one.

Eventually things hit the breaking point the night he sexually assaulted me. It was in April when the weather started to change a bit. In New York; it's never really that hot, but it was warm that day, so I didn't need a jacket. I wore a red button-up blouse, a black skirt, and heels. It was one of the many nights he had made me stay late. The office was empty that night. The office always closed at seven, and it was around nine. I had my back facing the door. I heard the door lock, and I turned around, and he was standing there. He looked me up and down for a few seconds and didn't say anything. Then it happened on that same black leather couch. Time was going by slowly, and it felt like forever. Afterward, I just sat there. I couldn't cry; I couldn't yell. I just sat there. He walked out of the office and didn't say anything or acknowledge me at all. I put my clothes on, and I left. I got back to my room.

Luckily my roommates were out that night. I went into the bathroom, and I just stared at myself in the mirror for a while. I immediately blamed myself. I tried to come up with a hundred possible reasons for why this could have happened, and there weren't any; it was not my fault, it couldn't have been. You always hear about these things and think, "it could never happen to you," until it does. I never thought this would happen. Then it hit me. I had a rush of all emotions hitting me at once. I broke down. I fell to the ground in tears. I wondered if the people next door could hear me. I covered my mouth as I sobbed. I could barely catch my breath. I took my clothes off, and something just told me to put my underwear in a Ziplock bag. I don't know why I thought that would help. I never thought this legal case would happen. I guess I just put them in there to hide it, lock it away, and try to forget. I looked in the mirror again. I saw myself covered in bruises, and I felt unrecognizable. I was a picture of a broken girl, away from home, away from her family, and all alone. I didn't have many friends, and I certainly couldn't speak of this to anyone on campus. The president of Morrid was the most respected man on campus. Everyone adored him and thought he was a good, solid guy. Who would believe me?

Days went by, and I hadn't left my room. I missed so much school to the point where I thought they would kick me out. I couldn't keep any food down, and I threw up way too much. The assault kept replaying in my mind. It was on a loop, like a never-ending merry-go-round. I was dizzy and sick. I couldn't even tell my mom yet. My mom was my best friend, and I knew she would try to make her way here immediately. I just wish she were here. So she could tell me everything was gonna be okay. It took me weeks to build up the courage to tell my mom. I made her promise to tell dad after I hung up, so I didn't have to.

Twenty days after the assault...

Veronica: Hi, Mom.

Mom: *Hola, mi amor. Inglés?*

Veronica: Is my English good?

Mom: I think so, yes.

Veronica: Mama, I miss you.

Mom: I miss you too! Your father is driving me crazy. He doesn't enjoy my shows.

Veronica: Well, I don't blame him; you and your shows are too much.

Mom: I suppose. Everything fun there? I have never been to the city.

Veronica: It's beautiful.

Mom: Tell me about your classes. What are they like?

Veronica: They're not too bad. Now that I've learned this language, classes are easier.

Mom: What classes are you taking? I forgot.

Veronica: English, statistics, intro to law, sociology, and economics.

Mom: Economics?

Veronica: It's a class that explores how people and firms produce and consume goods and services, supply, and demand. Stuff like that.

Mom: You like it?

Veronica: It's okay. It's just a lot of information.

Mom: Do you like your teachers?

Veronica: They're decent.

Mom: Not too hard?

Veronica: Not really, just fast paced. It's a lot of information.

Mom: No translation in class?

Veronica: No, I've just been trying to do without it now.

Mom: I'm impressed. Are you okay? Your voice sounds sad.

Veronica: Mama, I have to tell you something.

Mom: Is everything okay?

Veronica: No. Everything isn't okay.

Mom: Tell me.

Veronica: I was sexually assaulted.

Mom: Veronica, oh my god.

Veronica: It was the president of campus who did it.

Mom: The Spencer man? Is that the internship guy?

Veronica: Yes.

Mom: When did this happen?

Veronica: About three weeks ago. I didn't know how to say it out loud. I haven't been able to sleep, and I haven't gone to classes. I'm scared I'll see him.

Mom: Oh, baby, I'm so sorry this happened to you. How can I help? I cannot even imagine how much this is affecting you.

Veronica: I don't know what to do, Mom. I can't come home, then I can't come back.

Mom: Is staying there really worth it?

Veronica: I don't know, Mom. I may want to come home.

Mom: Say the words, and we can arrange that. Immediately.

Veronica: I just don't know what to do.

Mom: This breaks me. I'm so sorry.

Veronica: Mama, you've said sorry twice now.

Mom: I shouldn't have let you go so far.

Veronica: Mom, this could have happened anywhere.

Mom: I know, *mija*. I just can't hug you. I always wanted to protect you.

Veronica: I know, Mom.

Mom: Thank you for telling me about this. I hate that there's not more I can do.

Veronica: Me too. I don't even know where to go from here.

Mom: Take it one day at a time. Every day is a new day. We love you unconditionally, Veronica. I'm just one phone call away.

Veronica: I know; I love you guys too.

Mom: What about your father? You have not told him.

Veronica: Can you? I can't handle telling him.

Mom: I suppose I can. Keep me updated with everything. Take as much time off from classes as you need.

Veronica: Thanks, Mom.

Mom: Remember, this was not your fault. Call me if you need anything. I'll check on you more.

Veronica: Love you.

Mom: I love you more. Bye.

Telling my mom took everything out of me. I could tell that deep down she blamed herself for letting me come this far from home, but it wasn't her fault. There was no way we could have known this would happen. I just hated that she had to find out on a phone call. I could have only imagined my father's reaction to that. I'm sure he was furious. He told me I'd always be his little girl, no matter how old I got. Someone took advantage of his little girl, and I'm sure this broke him as much as it broke my mom.

Chapter Twenty-Eight

Dylan Spencer
Friday, November 11th, 7:30 p.m.

I had been dreading this game since the media got a hold of Marcus's arrest. I promised my coach I was okay to play, but now I'm not so sure. Everyone's been on the edge of their seats for this game. Brown has been our rival for decades. Knowing the spotlight is on me is making me feel overwhelmed. The pressure normally doesn't get to me; if anything, it's like adrenaline. Now it feels like I'm suffocating, like I'm waiting for the inevitable to happen. I've been in the stadium locker room for all of ten minutes, and I have never been so ready for a game to be over.

"Yo, Dylan? Are you good?" asked Michael.

"He looks green," chimed in Nick.

"I'm fine, guys. I'm ready to get this game over with," I said back.

"Come on, Dyl; we've been waiting on this game for months," said Michael.

"Are you sure you're okay, D? You seem different," said Nick.

"Different how?" I asked.

"Jumpy. Not really yourself at all," said Nick.

"Is this about your grandfather?" asked Michael.

"Don't call him that. His name is Marcus," I said, raising my voice.

"Why are you calling him by his name?" asked Nick.

"Well, it's his name, isn't it?" I sighed.

"Are you sure you're okay?" asked Michael.

"I guess," I answered.

"Did Mariah ever text you back, Mike?" asked Nick.

"Nope. I texted her two days ago. Guess she's not interested. I tried, man. I really did. I don't think it's gonna happen," said Michael.

"Sorry about that," I said.

"It's cool. I liked her, but I guess she doesn't feel the same way," Michael said.

"Wow," Nick said under his breath.

"Doesn't matter. The pro scouts reached out," Michael said with a shrug.

"No way. When?" asked Nick.

"About a week ago. They're out there tonight, so y'all better play your hearts out," Michael said.

I was happy for Michael. He's a good player, and he deserves to play for a good team. It's pretty impressive that the NFL scouts are interested in him. I hadn't paid much mind to going to the NFL. I guess it would be cool and something I could potentially be interested in. I just didn't really know if football was going to be in my future.

Time was passing by extremely fast. Before I knew it, I was suiting up for tonight's game, and I got a text that read, "Meet me outside. I have information. Detective Clark." I took a deep breath and continued tying my cleats. I grabbed my helmet and jogged outside the locker room. I got outside, and I saw him standing out there by the wall with our school's name in big letters, in our school colors of purple and gold. He's just standing there, looking around. I walked up to him, and he turned to face me.

"Dylan. Nice to see you," he said.

"Likewise." I shrugged.

"Is this how a rich school typically looks? I was expecting there to be trails of money," he joked.

"Okay, what is it?" I said, demanding answers.

"Hmmm. Not much for humor tonight, I see," he said.

"Not at all," I said.

"Well, I'm trying to lighten the mood because the information I found out is very dark," he said.

"Whatever it is, I'm sure I can take it," I said, setting my helmet down.

"I have reason to believe your grandfather is a part of a human trafficking circle. I was able to access an IP tracing back to him. There's a web that is accessible for offenders to sell and communicate with others. I believe your grandfather is the owner of the circle."

"A sex trafficking ring? I don't get it. How would he have the time to do that?" I asked.

"It's a lot more common than you think among public figures. People like him are well respected in their communities, which means victims are more likely to be manipulated by them. It also means he has connections, and I believe he is controlling one of the biggest trafficking rings in New York," he explained thoroughly.

"Explain to me his role in this. This trafficking thing," I asked.

"Each trafficker is different. The role your grandfather is most likely playing is controlling the circle. Meaning people most likely work for him. They go out and seek women, sometimes men, and they most likely check with him before the abduction. Making sure they fit his standards. They then upload photographs of these victims to a database where sexual predators can then bid on them," he explained.

"You think my old grandfather is doing this? That old man," I asked with doubt.

"Yes, I do. I can prove it. He's been purchasing women. I decided to cross-trace payments he's made over the past few years, and I got nothing at first. So then, I went deeper. I was able to find an account he has. This account has made payments up to $100,000. This was concerning, so I had to track where those payments were going. I found out that those payments have gone directly to a website that I cannot access," he explained.

"I don't even know what to say to that." I shrugged. "Have you ever noticed anything off about your grandfather? Aggression? Manipulation. Hyper sexualization of women," he questioned.

"Well, yes. He has always been violent when I was growing up. He would have violent outbursts and would shove me around a lot. He's a manipulator as well. He would lie and harass women," I said.

"I'll keep looking into this. I will let you know when I have an update. Would you like me to forward you the files I have?" he said.

"Yes, thank you," I said.

"Good luck at your game. I'll be in touch," he said.

My grandfather is not only an assaulter but potentially in charge of a trafficking ring. I have no words. I don't understand how sick a person could be. I truly am at a loss for words. What I can't believe is that he's allowed around my little sister. There's no telling what could have happened. The fact he is even allowed around my mother makes me sick. Now, I have to play the biggest game of the year after finding out that my grandfather is not only a sexual predator but also sells women to other sexual predators. I keep replaying that conversation in my head as I walk onto the field.

"Spencer, are you ready for this game?" asked Coach Parker.

"I don't know if I am, Coach," I said.

"The guys out there need you, Dylan," Coach said.

"I know, coach," I say as I put my helmet on.

"I didn't want to tell you before, but the NFL Patriots scout is out there tonight. Rumor has it they need a wide receiver, and apparently, they got their eyes on you," Coach explained.

"Really? How come you didn't tell me?" I asked.

"I didn't want to add to your stress. I knew you had a lot on your plate with everything going on," Coach said.

"Well, I appreciate it. Are they really here tonight?" I asked.

"Yes, they are," he answered.

"Coach, you should've told me," I said.

"Come on, Spencer. You think that would've been best?" Coach asked.

"Well, I don't know if it would've been for the best. But at least I would have known," I said.

"Can I give you some advice, Dylan?" Coach asked.

"Yeah, you can," I said.

"Stop blaming yourself for things you cannot control. You couldn't have known your grandfather would end up this way," he said.

"I guess, but I could have caught it sooner. His actions have always been this way," I said.

"What do you mean?" he asked.

"He's always been this way, coach. He isn't perfect. I wish people would stop pretending he was," I said.

"I think it's a lesson, son. Don't let anyone—family, friends, or lover—ever make you cruel. The actions of a person will tell you about who they are. I believe you're a good man, Dylan. Don't blame yourself for this. It'll tear you apart," he explained.

"How do I stop myself from thinking about it?" I asked.

"You have to understand there's bad people in this world. Not everyone has good intentions or a good heart," Coach said.

"I just hate for the girl to have had to go through this over something he's done. Do you think he's guilty, coach?" I asked.

"There's no telling, but I know that I always believe the victim. I have a wife and two daughters. I cannot imagine the constant fear that women endure. My only goal is to protect my girls and my wife with everything in me. Justice will be served; I have faith in that," he said.

"I remember you telling me about your girls. Isn't Isabelle seven?" I asked.

"She just turned eight last week. She's so sassy. She's just like her mother. Being the only man in the house is hard because they always gang up on me," he says with a bit of a laugh.

"My mom and sister are like that. My sister, Evie, is just like my mom. They mean the world to me," I said.

"Then do whatever you can to make them proud tonight. I'm sure they're going to watch it on TV," he said.

"I'll give it my all, Coach" I said.

"I know you will, Dylan. Now go out there and show the scouts you're ready for the draft in April," he says with a smile.

Chapter Twenty-Nine

Brooklyn Reed
Friday, November 11th, 8:45 p.m.

Dylan has been playing his heart out this entire game. I was worried that what's happening was going to affect him in the game. I think this has been one of his best games this whole season, and he's played extremely well in all the games. Dylan has never talked about what he wants to do after college. I always thought he'd just play football, but I don't really know. I could see him playing professionally or having something to do with coaching. He doesn't strike me as a typical football guy. He doesn't really make it his whole life or even really talk about it. A lot of the guys here are on social media with the team. I think Dylan only has pictures of me and Reese on his Instagram, and maybe one picture up with Michael and Nick after practice one time. I wish he talked about football more; I feel like I'm the one always talking, and he's the listener. He's always been that way, though—never much of a talker. Sometimes he's just in his own world, or he's just comforting me about something. I wish I could express to him how thankful I am for him. I'm sure I do, but sometimes it doesn't feel like enough. Dylan goes above and beyond for all of his friends, and it surprises me more every day. He deserves the absolute best in this world. I had always known Dylan was a good guy, but I think when we found out about the assault, I could truly tell what a good guy he was. He immediately believed Veronica when he could've been completely different about the whole thing. Dylan's not like every other guy. He's genuine; he's sweet. He doesn't care about superficial things or materialistic things. His family is extremely wealthy, and Dylan never advertises it. He doesn't even think much of it.

My mind has been running in circles thinking about this case. Now that Marcus is in custody, I'm sure Veronica's feeling overwhelmed, and it's going to be hard knowing her family is thousands of miles away. I looked down at my phone to see that JJ had called me a few minutes ago. I missed her call, so I'm going to call her back.

> Brooklyn: Hey, JJ, sorry I missed your call. What's up?
> JJ: Sorry to call on a Friday night, but we have a court date scheduled.
> Brooklyn: For when?
> JJ: November 21st.
> Brooklyn: Wow, that's soon.
> JJ: Yeah, they told me a little bit ago. I called Veronica to tell her. She seemed nervous when I told her.
> Brooklyn: How was there a court date so soon?

JJ: I'm not sure. It could be the fact that he's a public figure. Cases like these are usually rushed into court.

Brooklyn: So what does this mean for Veronica?

JJ: Well, she's not the one on trial here; he is. She will read the closing statement at the end and be asked a few questions and such.

Brooklyn: Did she say she would do it?

JJ: Yes, actually. She told me she was ready.

Brooklyn: Really?

JJ: Yes, she sounded nervous but fired up at the same time. I guess, after a while, she's not as scared to face him anymore. She's so strong.

Brooklyn: Do you know her chances as far as winning this?

JJ: I'm not sure. Marcus being a lawyer is going to make this very tricky. I made the people aware of this, mostly about his close relationships to other lawyers and judges. So, they promised to get another judge from out of state. But due to how well known he is, I recommend a jury. It most likely would be better for her to have a jury rather than a judge.

Brooklyn: She's allowed to decide that stuff?

JJ: Partially yes, but Marcus has to agree to it.

Brooklyn: I don't think he will.

JJ: Maybe not, but I can push for one.

Brooklyn: Are you able to do that?

JJ: Yes, I can just say how I want it to be a fair trial and that his close ties to other judges could compromise the integrity of the trial.

Brooklyn: That might be best.

JJ: I'll call first thing Monday.

Brooklyn: Sounds good, JJ. Thank you.

JJ: Of course. Talk to you then.

Brooklyn: Talk to you soon.

Chapter Thirty

Dylan Spencer
Monday, November 14th, 9:30 a.m.

The weekend flew by. I slept practically the whole weekend and ordered in. I talked to Brooklyn on and off, but she's been sort of in her own world about things. I have class in a few. My mind has been scattered. I totally spaced about my book report. I don't even know what's going on with me. I've been skipping class, not eating, and missing assignments left and right. It's only a matter of time before my coach finds out if he hasn't already. I've had enough going on with this stalker, the assault, the sex trafficking, school, and everything else. I also got to stop by Lucas's office to see if he found anything I needed to know.

After rushing to get to class, I still managed to be ten minutes late. I sat in the whole class and completely paid zero attention.

"Dylan, you're up next to present your report," said Professor Claire.

"Sorry, I don't have it," I said.

"No report? No presentation?" she asked.

"No, sorry," I said.

"Okay, does anyone else have theirs?" she asked the class.

A few people raised their hands, but it wasn't much of the class. I couldn't understand the point of a book presentation. It seemed useless. She gives us the most useless assignments. I'm not complaining about the reading or the books, just the reports. Every other week, we have these. We've been reading *Of Mice and Men*; it's an interesting story. We're at the part where Lennie kills Curley's wife, and he runs away. It's a book that has kept me engaged. I just forgot about the book report. The book report is basically a summary of the chapter, our thoughts, and how we interpret it. It's a pretty easy assignment, so I just forgot about it. Which reminded me of something else I forgot to do. I forgot to wish Brooklyn "good luck" on her presentation today.

After class ended, I tried to dash to the door, but Professor Claire stopped me before I could make it out.

"Dylan, do you think we can have a quick chat?" she asked kindly.

"Yeah, sure," I said, making my way back into the classroom.

"Is everything okay? I know a lot is going on with the controversial situation with your family," she asked.

"Not family; it's just Marcus. What about it?" I said back.

"I don't mean to pry, but do you need time to get this report done? I'd hate for you to lose points. We don't do exams here, so these weigh pretty heavily," she said.

"So what do you recommend I do?" I asked.

"I recommend doing it. Your writing is so good, Dylan. I really enjoy all the essays and reports you do. You really do have a gift with that. If you decide football is not just all you want to do," she said.

"Thanks, I guess. I'll get to it then," I say.

"When can I expect it to be done?" she asks.

"I'm not sure. I got practice and stuff," I say.

"Well, Dylan, you currently have an A in here. It would most likely remain an A. But I checked your grades and saw an issue. You have a D in statistics, which will put you on academic probation," she says.

"What? How do I have a D?" I asked.

"I would go talk to your professor to find the answer to that question. Anything below a C will get you suspended from the team. You have amazing grades, but you have to pull up statistics" she explained.

"Thanks for letting me know. I'll have the report to you by Friday at the latest," I said.

I take a deep breath, and I walk out of the room. I walk upstairs, which is where my math professor's office is. I peek in there and see Professor Zayne sitting at his desk. To be completely honest, I'm nervous. I didn't think my grade had dropped that much, if at all. It was a B the last time I checked. I walked into his office, and he's sitting there typing on the computer.

"Dylan Spencer, a pleasure to see you finally. What brings you here?" he asked.

"I'm here about my grade, which is currently a D," I said.

"Hmm, that might be because you missed the last exam. An away game, I guess? I am more than welcome to let you make up the exam. Although that exam was almost a month ago and you hadn't come to take it. I'd let you take it, but I will take 15 percent off," he explained.

"When can I do it?" I asked.

"How about next week, Monday? I will have an opening," he explained.

"Okay, sounds good," I said.

"Are you available for tutoring this week to prepare?" he asked.

"I'm not sure. I do weight lifting every day and have practice," I said.

"You may have to reach out to a classmate," he said.

"A classmate? I don't know anyone there," I said.

"You don't really talk to anyone in there either. I'm not sure what to tell you," he said.

"Who do you recommend?" I asked.

"Everyone is doing pretty well; as far as the concepts from last month, I'm not sure," he said.

"You could go to the math center? They meet every other day at 8:00 a.m.," he said.

"I have my practices in the mornings, so that isn't going to work," I said.

"Well, that's a practice you may have to miss," he said.

"If I miss practice, I don't get to play," I said.

"Well, Dylan, if you don't do well on this test, you won't be doing football at all for the rest of the year. Wouldn't you rather sacrifice one game instead of the whole rest of the season?" he asked.

"I guess. When are you available to tutor?" I asked.

"I am available by booking. Unfortunately, I am booked up this week. So I am unsure if I will be able to help," he said.

Now what am I gonna do? My schedule doesn't allow me to do anything, and now one of my grades is dropping because of it. If I miss practice, I can't play at the game. This week is an important one. We play Manhattan College, and the scouts are going to be there. But next week, if I fail this exam, I won't be on the team at all. So that means I'm going to have to figure something out, and soon or else I'll be on academic probation and done for the season.

Chapter Thirty-One

Brooklyn Reed
Monday, November 14th, 10:00 a.m.

Today is a day that I have been dreading for a few weeks. In sociology, each of us has a debate topic, and the whole class gets involved. I hate presenting in class; I get so nervous. For this presentation, it has to be controversial to spark a discussion and "free thinking." I'm next up to go. I haven't heard from Dylan all morning, which is weird. He usually texts me first thing, but I guess it must've just slipped his mind.

"Brooklyn, you're next up," said Professor Laurence.

I take a deep breath, get up from my seat, and walk to the front of the classroom with my notes.

"My topic is how prejudice plays into the treatment minorities receive in healthcare. In society, a doctor's job is to heal and nurture. When doctors begin to abuse their power and act on personal prejudice, that is when a significant problem begins to occur. As a whole, issues revolving around personal prejudice should not affect the care a person receives.

Personal prejudice shouldn't be to the extent to which a life is lost or put in danger," I explained to the class.

In the distance, I can sense this is going to spur up a pretty heavy discussion, and there it goes; a hand goes up. It's Lewis. Lewis always contributes nothing to these discussions. I can sense that not only is he going to say something arrogant, but it will also be something that's going to enrage me.

"Yes, Lewis. Do you have a question?" I asked.

"Yeah, I guess I could say it's a question. How exactly is this proven to be true? I mean, what factors could there even be? What proof is there to be?" he asked all in one breath.

"Language proficiency, errors associated with formal and informal interpretation, misinterpretation of instructions, income, insurance, beliefs about illness and treatment, family and friends for safety vigilance, and patient-professional behavior. While all these factors are important, the main factor is language proficiency. Language barriers are enough of an issue on their own in health care," I explain with an eye roll at the end.

"Correct me if I'm wrong. Last time I checked, people are trying to fix the language barrier," he said.

"Okay, but that doesn't dismiss the fact that there is a huge lack of communication, which can pose a bigger threat regarding discussions between doctors and patients about prescription drugs. Yes, people have hired bilingual health care staff, and this shifted things into a positive change," I explained.

"Honestly, Lewis, if you think realistically that this issue doesn't exist, not only are you stupider than we all thought you were, but you are part of the problem," said Madelynn.

I'm going to be honest; I didn't expect Madelynn to really agree with my side at all. She's opinionated, and she sort of reminds me of those mean girls from the movie, but that girl just surprised me. I guess I've got to learn the concept of not judging a book by its cover. I was expecting her to completely shut me down and side with Lewis. She never really says anything in class, but I've heard her talk outside of class, and you can tell when someone is raised with privilege. Her parents are pretty wealthy. I'm not really sure what jobs they have, but I know she drives a white Range Rover. I guess I've got her all wrong. She may not be that bad of a person.

Chapter Thirty-Two

Dylan Spencer
Monday, November 14th, 4:00 p.m.

I decided to check in with Lucas to see if he'd found anything. I haven't been able to get the German connection and the message "continue to play" out of my mind. It was so random, and it felt like it was some code or something. A code that I wasn't going to be able to figure out on my own. Lucas was really my only hope. I could tell he didn't like me too much, but he's been very helpful in his own way. So, I figured I'd pay him a quick visit. When I walked into his office, I noticed he had on black beats and was listening to music.

"Hey, Lucas," I said loudly as I walk into his office.

"Dylan Spencer. I was just about to call you," Lucas said as he takes off his headphones.

"Found something?" I asked.

"Is five the fifth digit in the pi number?" Lucas asked.

"Huh?" I said.

"Yes, the answer is yes; I found something," Lucas says with an eye roll.

"How the hell was I supposed to know that?" I asked.

"You take calculus, don't you?" Lucas asked.

"No, I take statistics," I said.

"That class is pretty simple. Is that why you take it?" Lucas asked.

"I'm not in the mood. What did you find out?" I asked, crossing my arms.

"Remember you were curious about the whole German thing? Turns out one of the school's biggest donors is a German education group. I tried to dig more on them, but it was a simple search. It turns out they fund different things in education, such as colleges that lost funding previously, but the weirdest thing is they always get paid back. Their services seem more like an exchange than funding," Lucas explained.

"That doesn't really make sense though. Why would a place in Germany be funding our school, and why would we pay back? How would they even know of our school?" I ask.

"It says a man named Karl Walter is in charge of these fundings for colleges, and he usually picks and chooses them," Lucas said.

"Karl Walter," I repeated numerous times.

"You know him?" Lucas asked.

"Why does that name sound so familiar?" I asked.

"Could be because he was on the news about two years ago. It says here that he was under investigation for having child pornography. Says here that they even found evidence of it. Allegedly, he wasn't sent to trial and pretty much paid this whole thing off," Lucas explains.

"Why does our school still receive this funding?" I asked.

"It says here that your grandfather and him were close friends back in the day," Lucas said.

"That doesn't surprise me at all," I said.

"What do you mean?" asked Lucas.

"Nothing. I don't understand how the school allowed him to do it," I said.

"Well, technically, they most likely don't care as long as they're getting funding," Lucas said.

"Why wouldn't they care? He's a predator," I said.

"Well, to the school, he's just a bank, giving them money without any question. It says here he's been funding the school for ten years. That's weird; that's how long your grandfather has been president," Lucas explained.

"Yeah, it is. I just don't get it," I said.

"Honestly, I think Morrid has been sketchy ever since he got here. No offense," Lucas said.

"Trust me, no offense taken. Tell me about the sketchy stuff," I said.

"Well, for starters, the school's financial record is concerning. The amount of money that has been exchanged should be illegal for a private school. I've tried to access this information, but I can't do it without the password. It's practically locked up, even sealed. I guess the president didn't want anyone to access the financial records of the university," Lucas said.

"But why would these files be a secret? Shouldn't there at least be a track record of these things?" I asked.

"Well, there should be. These things are required, especially for checking fraud reports and such. There's got to be a way to access this information," Lucas said.

"Would only the president know the code?" I asked.

"Most likely yes. It's only a three digit code, but those files are most likely in a safe in his office," Lucas said.

"Only three digits?" I asked.

"Yeah. Most codes here are either three digits or six. Though they have strict security over these codes. Only the president knows them or people in the office," Lucas said.

"How would someone be able to access the files without the code?" I asked.

"The code is the only way. The files are in a safe box in his office, Dylan; it'll be nearly impossible to even get into his office without a key," Lucas said.

"Nearly impossible, not just impossible. There's got to be a way," I said.

"Do you think you know any of the interns there? They could potentially have a key, but I doubt it. I don't think he just gives the key out," Lucas said.

"There might be a chance he did. I guess I'll have to look into it," I said.

"Just be careful. There's no telling what security there is in the president's building, especially since the arrest," Lucas said.

"Yeah, you're right. Thanks for your help, man," I said.

"Anytime, I'm gonna need an additional one hundred," Lucas begged.

"Why? I just paid the price the other day," I said.

"I've got to eat." He shrugged.

"I'll cash app you," I said, walking out of his office.

This left me wondering how to find this code and, most importantly, how to get into his office. He'd most likely be the only one with a key. I knew what I had to do, and I had to break into his office tonight. The only way I was going to be able to do that was if Brooklyn got the key from Veronica and I figured out the pin for the safe box. So this plan was going to require me telling Brooklyn everything I've found out.

Chapter Thirty-Three

Brooklyn Reed
Monday, November 14th, 7:30 p.m.

"Hey, Dylan, haven't heard from you all day," I said as he walked into my apartment.

"Sorry, I found out a lot today. Is Mariah here?" Dylan asked as he looked around.

"No, she's still in Boston. She decided to stay until after Thanksgiving break," I answered.

"But break doesn't start till the 22nd," Dylan said.

"Have you met Mariah? Her breaks always start a week early," I said.

"Yeah, that does sound like her," Dylan said with a laugh.

"What brings you here, Dyl?" I asked.

"I have a lot to tell you, Brookie. Can we sit?" Dylan said seriously.

"Yeah, of course. What's going on?" I asked.

"Okay, keep in mind I haven't told you this stuff because it's still pretty new to me too," Dylan explained.

"What is it?" I asked restlessly.

"I hired a PI to dig into Marcus's money laundering, which my dad told me about. The PI told me the other night he found evidence of sex trafficking and believes Marcus is over this whole sex trafficking ring. Then I found out tonight from a friend here that Marcus is friends with this German guy whose company funds our school. This guy is basically a child predator. Anyway there's a chance the school is covering up some sketchy stuff," Dylan explained.

"Dylan, what?" I asked.

"That's not all. There's a lot more," Dylan said with a sigh.

Dylan was right. There was a lot more. Not only did he not tell me he had a stalker, but he didn't tell me this person was watching me too. I'm upset he didn't tell me, but I understand he did this to keep me safe. I wanted to tell him about the photograph on the security camera, but I decided not to. I can't help but wonder why Mariah got to know. I guess it made sense to him at the time, but it makes me sad. I don't understand why he wanted to go through this alone, without any moral support. He said Reese doesn't know either, which I didn't expect him to tell Reese. But me? I'm his girlfriend. I thought he could tell me anything. His whole explanation of things took about an hour. He mentioned the messages he received, the photographs, the letters, and how this person knew about German. I still don't fully understand the way Lucas fits into this whole thing. I didn't even know Dylan knew who Lucas was. Dylan did seem spooked talking about the whole thing.

"Sorry, I didn't tell you sooner. I thought it would cause more harm than good," Dylan said.

"I understand, Dylan. I'm not mad. I'm just worried. Someone knows where your family lives. Does that scare you?" I asked.

"It does scare me very much. I just don't know what to do. Especially now that it's escalated to all this actual criminal stuff. I think all this, even the stalking, has to do with Marcus," Dylan explained.

"You think your grandfather knows who's stalking you?" I asked.

"He's got to. Why else would they call Veronica a liar?" Dylan said.

"You make a good point." I shrugged.

"I have a favor for you," Dylan said.

"What's the favor?" I asked.

"Can you ask Veronica if she still has the key to his office?" Dylan asked.

"Dylan, are you crazy? Why would I ask her that?" I groaned.

"So, we can break into his office and find the files, Brookie. Please," Dylan said, begging almost.

"I don't like this idea at all," I said.

"Brooklyn, please," Dylan begged.

"Fine. I'll text and ask her," I said hesitantly.

> *9:45 p.m.*
> Brooklyn: Hey, Veronica. Quick question.
> Veronica: Hey, Brooklyn. What's up?
> Brooklyn: Do you, by any chance, still have the key to the president's office?
> Veronica: Yeah, I never came back to return it. Why?
> Brooklyn: Do you think I could borrow it?
> Veronica: What for?
> Brooklyn: I can't necessarily say.
> Veronica: Something illegal, I'm guessing.

Brooklyn: Well, yes.

Veronica: Is everything okay?

Brooklyn: Well, I think so.

Veronica: What's going on?

Brooklyn: My boyfriend is acting like he is Sherlock Holmes.

Veronica: Lol. Just be safe.

Brooklyn: I'll try my best.

Veronica: You can stop by and get it. I'm in West Hardin Dorm, second floor, 235.

Brooklyn: Thanks! Be there in five.

Veronica: Okay!

I take a deep breath and try to imagine that my boyfriend and I aren't about to commit the crime of breaking and entering. It feels almost unreal. If I asked myself two years ago if I'd be breaking into the president's office to find the answers to questions that I didn't even know existed two hours ago, I'd be shocked. Not only does Dylan find out all this information and tell me about it today, but he also plans to break into the office tonight, and he wants me to join him. I guess I should be happy that he trusted me with this information and wanted me to tag along with him.

After getting the key from Veronica, Dylan and I headed to the President's building, but instead of walking there, Dylan said we should drive, just in case we have to make a "run for it." Why won't Dylan just get the police involved? I don't even know.

"Dylan, are you sure we should do this?" I asked.

"I'm positive. You're more than welcome to stay in the car," Dylan said.

"No, Dylan," I protested.

"Then please don't second-guess this," Dylan said seriously.

"I just don't understand why you can't tell the police." I sighed.

"Do you really think that's the best idea?" Dylan asked sarcastically.

"We don't even have a plan, Dylan," I said.

"Okay, well, give me a second to think of one," Dylan said.

"Did you even take into account security cameras?" I asked.

"No, I did not. Shoot," Dylan said.

"Good thing I did. Here's a hat," I say as I give him a pink hat.

"Pink, really?" Dylan complained.

"You're really going to complain now? Put the hat on," I said.

"Fine," Dylan said as he puts on the hot pink hat.

"See, you look cute," I said as I chuckled.

"Whatever. We go inside, I unlock the door and look for the safe box. You stand out of the office and keep guard," Dylan explained.

"Keep guard? Are we in an episode of *Law and Order*?" I say with a laugh.

"Brooklyn, please." Dylan begged.

Truthfully, I couldn't take him seriously in that bright pink hat. I knew he was gonna hate it; that's why I brought it. It reminded me of the time I painted Dylan's nails. It was a few weeks after we started dating, and Dylan practically lived over at my place. He would usually stay the night because we'd be up watching movies. It was one night before one of the biggest games. I'm not sure who they played that night, but I'm sure it was a pretty good team. Dylan was pacing across the room, telling me about how nervous he was for this game. I was pretty sure it was one of the only games I had seen Dylan get so worked up over. So I told him he should let me paint his nails hot pink. He instantly refused, of course. Then I begged him, and I told him he'd love it, and it'd be like a good luck charm. Plus, I just wanted him to sit still. It took some convincing, but eventually he came around and let me paint his nails pink. He wouldn't stay still while I did it. He kept complaining that the polish was "cold." I knew he was being dramatic, so I just ignored his complaining.

When I finished his nails, he said, "I can't believe I let you talk me into this." I knew deep down that he loved it. He complained about his nails the whole night until we went to bed.

The next day, at the game, he did extremely well. It was half-time when he looked up at the crowd and saw me. I've always sat at the same place since his very first game, so he'd be able to find me easily among the crowd of people. He took his gloves off and waved at me. He then held up a heart symbol with his hands and pointed to his nails in pink. It was the cutest thing I had ever seen. I knew at that moment the nail polish color that he "hated," he actually loved. It makes me happy that he even acknowledges me at the games. I'm sure his mind is so busy during those games, but he will still look for me. Now, years later, Dylan still waves at me and holds up a heart symbol with his hands. It makes me feel so full of love, love that I can't even contain. It leaves me wondering how I got so lucky with him.

"Brookie? Are you ready to go in?" Dylan asked.

I must have zoned out. "Sorry, I was just thinking. I'm ready," I said.

We got out of the car and made our way into the president's building, which was by far the nicest building on campus. I had never been in this building before. I was amazed. It wasn't anything like I pictured it would be. I thought it'd look boring and be filled with desks and such. But it wasn't anything like that at all. It looked so modern and unique. Everything was practically made of glass, and it was like something out of those fancy movies. Dylan and I walked around very quietly, trying not to make a sound. We got to the president's office, and it was huge. You could see the inside of the office from the hall because everything was made out of glass; it was stunning.

"I'm gonna put the key in and go in, but you have to stay out here," Dylan said.

"But, Dylan, I wanna go in. There's no one here," I said.

"I know, Brooklyn, but just in case," Dylan said.

"What do I do if someone comes, though?" I asked.

"Well, if you hear them coming before they see you, then just tell me, and we'll make a run for it," Dylan explained.

"So, what if they see me? What do we do then?" I asked.

"Then we'd have to come up with a lie. Say how I'm his grandson, and I had to get some papers for him," Dylan said.

"So, I can't help at all?" I asked.

"You're helping right now, Brooklyn. Just stay right here," Dylan demanded.

"Okay. I'll stay here." I sighed.

Chapter Thirty-Four

Dylan Spencer
Monday, November 14th, 11:15 p.m.

I'm sure there could have been a better plan than breaking and entering, but this is what it has come to. I had Brooklyn stand outside his office and keep guard just in case anyone came. Also, a part of me didn't want her to see what I found before I saw it. Telling Brooklyn about this whole thing wasn't ideal. My goal was for her not to know anything, not until I figured out what this "thing" is. At first, I thought I would be able to find information about his money laundering. I didn't expect to find out he was in a trafficking ring and that one of his "accomplices" was a big donor for the school. It makes me wonder what other secrets he has been hiding.

When I entered his office, it had been very neat; nothing was out of place. It looked as though he had worked from home the last few days before his arrest, like he was prepared. When I first looked in his coat closet, I didn't find anything except for a receipt from a restaurant in the city. I decided to look in the other part of the closet. His closet was a multi-organizer closet; at least that's what Brooklyn calls them. It has a place for the coat and shoes, and even a drawer attached to hold things like clothes. In the drawer part, I couldn't find anything incriminating. There were only ties and socks in there, neatly placed. I continued to look around and headed to his desk. To my surprise, the desk drawers were sealed shut. There was no way to open them up either, like they were completely shut, which meant there was most likely something in there, or he just hadn't used them and left them that way. I decided to move over to the safe behind his desk. I'm guessing this is where Lucas said I'd most likely be able to find the financial records because it's safe. It blows my mind that he sealed something like the financial records. I figured things like this the people in the student office would have. Regardless, it was useless. I didn't have the code, and I didn't have any clue about how to get it. I decided to ask Brooklyn. If anyone could solve something like that, it was her.

"Brooklyn, come in here," I whispered.

"Everything okay? she asked.

"I can't figure out this code. It's three digits," I said.

"The code is three digits?" she asked.

"Yes," I said.

"That's weird; most of them are usually six. How did you know it was three?" she asked.

"Lucas told me," I said.

"How does Lucas know that?" she asked.

"I'm not sure," I said.

"Hmmm," she sighed.

"Can you help me figure out the code?" I asked.

"Yeah, of course. Any important messages you got from whoever has been stalking you. Any weird texts or something?" she asked.

"I got things like 'liar' and 'never believe a liar,'" I explained.

"I don't think he'd make it something as simple as one, two, or three," she says.

"I don't know what it could be," I said.

"Have you gotten any messages with three words?" she asks.

"I don't think so," I said.

"Think hard. It could've been a phrase or something," she said.

"Now that I think of it, there was a code in the database," I said, trying to think of what exactly it said.

"What type of code?" she asked.

"It was something in German. I don't know. Lucas said it translated to something like 'continue to play' or 'game on.'" I explained.

"Okay, so 'game on' is only two words," she said.

"'Continue to play' is three words," I said.

"Wait a minute. 'Continue' is eight. 'To' is two. 'Play' is four," she said.

"So that's the code?" I asked.

"Try eight-two-four," she suggested.

"It worked," I said.

"See anything in there? Dylan?" she asked.

"You've got to be kidding me," I said.

"What is it?" she asked.

"It's two things. One envelope and a sheet of white paper," I said.

"What does the paper say?" she asked.

"You were a little too late," I read.

"Let me open the envelope," she says and begins to open it. "Wow, Dylan. Your grandfather really didn't want you at the school," she said, glancing over the letter.

"What do you mean?" I asked.

"This is a letter that he wrote to your coach," said Brooklyn.

"What does it say?" I asked.

"Dear, Henry Parker. I'm writing this letter regarding my grandson, Dylan Spencer, who was offered a scholarship and a spot here on the team. It's come to my attention that he has gotten the attention of quite a few schools. I was notified you approached him at a high school game, and he committed here a few weeks ago. I'm coming to you as your president and request that you take back this offer. Regards, Marcus Spencer," Brooklyn read.

"Wow. He really didn't want me here," I said in disbelief.

"Yeah, that's what it sounds like," she said.

"Then why did he get Reese and I that suite? Why did he do those things?" I asked.

"I have no idea. But why would this be in the safe?" she asked.

"I have no idea," I said.

"Do you think whoever left the message got here first?" she asked.

"There's a chance of that," I said.

"Did you check the drawers?" she asked.

"Yeah, they were sealed," I said.

"Sealed?" she asked.

"Yeah, I couldn't open them," I said.

"Do you think he did that on purpose?" she asked.

"There's a chance, but there could also be nothing in there," I said.

"I don't think it'd be sealed if it were empty, Dyl. I think he's hiding something in there," she explained.

"Like what?" I asked.

"I don't know; it could be anything. We have to open it," she stated.

"How, Brookie? It's sealed shut," I said, tugging at the drawer.

"You can always unseal something if you find the way it's sealed," she said.

"Okay, how do we do that?" I asked.

"By looking at it, it doesn't seem sealed. It seems jammed," she said, looking at the drawer.

"Jammed, how?" I asked.

"Could be too much stuff in the drawer. Or it's rusty, so it's stuck," Brooklyn said.

"How do we get it out?" I said.

"Wait, is there soap?" she asked.

"Brooklyn, why would I need soap right now?" I asked.

"To loosen up the rust, Dylan. Trust me," she said.

"Yeah, I'm sure there's some in the bathroom," I say.

"Hurry and find some," she demanded.

I head to the bathroom, and I see a bottle of soap. "Found some. It's a liquid soap," I said, walking back to the office.

"That's perfect. Now look how I pour it in the creases, so it can get slippery. Okay, see if you can open it now," Brooklyn explained.

"It's working," I said with a smile.

"What's that in there?" she asked.

"It looks like a journal," I said.

"Open it," she said.

"Wait, I think it's a ledger," I said.

"Why would he just have that here? Shouldn't it be at his house or something?" Brooklyn asked.

"Maybe he put it here in case they searched his house," I said.

"Okay, let's take it with us and look through it tonight," she said.

"Can we look at it now? There's no telling what could be in here," I explained.

"If you want," she said.

"Wow, there's hundreds of transactions in here," I said.

"What kind of transactions?" she asked.

"I don't know, but everything is in huge amounts," I said.

"How huge?" she asked.

"It says $20,000, $5,000, and there's even $40,000 in here," I said.

"Wow…That's a lot of money," Brooklyn said, looking in the drawer.

"There's something illegal going on. This book may be able to prove that," I explained.

Chapter Thirty-Five

Brooklyn Reed
Tuesday, November 15th, 10:30 a.m.

ast night, Dylan and I found out a lot. His grandfather is a really sketchy guy. I mean, I get that he is very financially wealthy, but constant transactions of $20,000? That seems a bit extreme. People only make transactions that big constantly if they're doing something bad. We know he is involved in trafficking, but I don't think he'd just have proof of money transactions like that lying around, especially not in his place of work. I feel like we found it too easily. Dylan left the book with me since it's clear whoever is stalking him is getting their hands on his things. It's important we keep this book hidden because it could potentially be evidence. I'd been so preoccupied with this and the case that I haven't really checked on Mariah much since she went home two weeks early. I kind of miss her. I wish I could tell her about everything and just hear her thoughts. When I look around our apartment, it just seems so empty. Her clothes and fabric aren't just lying everywhere, and I don't hear opera in the background. Yes, opera. Mariah listens to it religiously. She said opera calms her down and gets rid of stress bumps. I don't really know what she is stressing about, considering she takes only, like, three classes. Most people are required to take at least six classes. I take six classes: Spanish, organic chemistry, neuroscience lecture and lab, sociology, and literature. All of which drive me completely insane. My homework to do list for this week consists of:

1. Finish "To Kill a Mockingbird" by Harper Lee by Friday for a test.
2. Start the chapter on deviance for sociology.
3. Complete the structures and bonding homework for organic chemistry.
4. Study for the biology exam on Thursday.
5. Finish lab report by Friday.

Luckily, I am finished with Spanish until after Thanksgiving break. Initially I planned to go home Friday after my literature test, but court will happen on Monday, the 21st. I really want to be in court to offer support for Veronica. I still don't know how she feels about this whole thing. She's putting on a strong face, but I can tell she's terrified. She has to see Marcus in court, and I can only imagine how traumatizing that's going to be for her. This week, she's not going to be communicating much because she's preparing her big closing statement. She's not letting me know what her statement says, so I won't know until court on Monday morning. I remember Veronica mentioning how lonely she felt here since her family is back in Cuba. It makes me want to bring her family here to New York City, so they can be here for the trial to support her and help bring her some comfort. I'm going to call JJ to ask what can be done to arrange that.

Brooklyn: Hey, JJ.

JJ: Hey, Brooklyn. What's up?

Brooklyn: I have a question. I'm not sure how possible this is.

JJ: What's your question?

Brooklyn: So Veronica has a big family, but they are in Cuba. What are the chances we can get them here by Monday morning?

JJ: Do they have visas?

Brooklyn: I don't think so. I know Veronica does.

JJ: It depends on how long they stay. They can stay a few days with only a passport. It may be tricky to stay longer without a visa.

Brooklyn: So the only thing they need is a passport and money for a plane ticket?

JJ: Do they have passports?

Brooklyn: I'm not sure. I don't have a way to contact them.

JJ: Luckily, I can. Her mom's number is in her file for her emergency contact.

Brooklyn: You will call her?

JJ: Of course.

Brooklyn: I'm not sure they'll be able to pay for it.

JJ: It says here that the cheapest flight from Havana, Cuba, to New York City is about $282. I can pay for those.

Brooklyn: JJ, are you sure? Tickets for her mom and dad?

JJ: Yes, I don't mind.

Brooklyn: Thank you, JJ.

JJ: Of course. She deserves it. She should be
able to see her family that day.

I admired JJ. The way she's doing everything she can for
Veronica is so inspiring. It makes me wonder why she's so passionate about this. I wasn't going to ask because I feel like
that's too personal. I'm grateful for Dylan because if it weren't
for him, we wouldn't have been able to meet JJ.

Chapter Thirty-Six

Reese Woods
Wednesday, November 16th, 3:00 p.m.

I finally finished every important class for this week. Classes like math and English don't count to me. On top of those classes, I just take interior design and two art classes. My semester was pretty light, and I wanted that to happen. Mariah had the right idea, leaving two weeks early. She was sort of bummed that she couldn't go to Cancun. She says they go every year. I had never been to Cancun before, and it's one of the places I really want to travel to. I would take Nick there. Nick hasn't traveled much growing up, and if he did travel, he said it was for football only. Nick and I have been good lately. He's been honest and open with me. It still feels unreal. It feels like a dream I'm going to wake up from. I've been learning more about him as the days have gone by, things like:

1. His favorite show is Friends.
2. His sister Avery is, like, his best friend; she's eighteen.
3. His parents don't know he's bi; only Avery does.
4. He likes blue Jolly Ranchers.

5. He's scared of small spaces.
6. He likes horror movies.
7. He doesn't like being alone.
8. He enjoys thunderstorms.
9. He loves to listen to rap music.
10. He gets nervous around people he doesn't really know.

I had been on and off with Nick for months, and it took me that long to be able to name ten things about him. I guess it's better late than never. I also know that Dylan and Michael are like brothers and have been since freshman year. I remember them always coming over, like every day. I used to hate it at first. Then I started to like Nick. Dylan didn't know about that for the longest time; I was sort of scared to tell him. I know how protective Dylan is, and I didn't want things to go crazy. Especially with the way Nick treated me for a while, I didn't tell Dylan about Nick for the longest time. I knew Dylan would try to "handle" it or say something to Nick about it. I didn't want to get him involved. More importantly, I didn't want to ruin my chances with Nick. No one knew about Nick and me except for Mariah, and I didn't tell her; she found out. One night she stopped by, and Nick was over. I didn't even say anything; she just put two and two together. Mariah's smart like that. I know we all pick on her for being a little ditsy, but she really does have a lot of sense.

As I was about to enter Dylan and my suite, I saw a package. I know for a fact that I didn't order anything. So, I pick up the package, and sure enough, it has Dylan's name on it. I pick the package up, and I unlock the door to get in. When I walk in, I see Dylan sitting in the living room, watching something on the television.

"Dylan, there's a package here for you," I announced.

He looked over at me and said, "I didn't order anything, though."

I walk over and hand him the package. He begins to open the package, and it's a bunch of papers.

"What is it, Dylan?" I asked.

"Information about the draft," Dylan said.

"What is a draft?" I asked.

"For the NFL, Reese," Dylan said with a laugh.

"I don't understand; you're still in college," I said, looking at the box.

"Yeah, but I'm a junior. You only got to be in college for three years to be considered for the draft," Dylan explained.

"Did you expect it?" I asked.

"Yeah, I had a feeling it was coming. Coach Parker told me the Patriots scouts were at the Brown game," Dylan said.

"The Patriots? Are they in Massachusetts?" I asked.

"Yeah, they are," Dylan said.

"You would leave us?" I asked.

"Don't say it like that, Reese. I don't know what I want to do," Dylan said.

"Well, what are you passionate about?" I asked.

"Well, I like to help people, and I like football," Dylan said.

"Would you say that football is your passion?" I asked.

"I mean, I guess. I've been doing it for a while. It's sort of my routine," Dylan explained.

"But do you love it, Dylan?" I asked.

"Your major is mass communications, right?" I asked.

"Yeah. I planned to do something like journalism in sports or something, but I don't know," Dylan said.

"Well, I wouldn't rule out doing the NFL, Dylan. You might regret it," I said.

"I guess you're right," Dylan said.

"You are going to be in the draft, right?" I said.

"Yeah, I want to. Could be fun," Dylan said.

"You'll be great, Dyl," I said.

"Thanks, Reese. I'm gonna head to get some food; are you coming?" Dylan asked.

"I'm sure it's fast food, so no," I said, crossing my arms.

"Alright, see you later." Dylan laughed.

"See ya," I said.

Chapter Thirty-Seven

Veronica Álvarez
Thursday, November 17th, 3:00 p.m.

The court date is slowly approaching, and I'm so nervous. JJ wanted me to call her today since she won't be able to talk to me before court. I've never even been in a courtroom before. JJ wants to walk me through the whole process. She says that Marcus's attorney will try to rip me apart and may even bring up my visa. In the American television shows I've seen, court is chaotic, and there's yelling sometimes. I don't know how I'm going to be able to do this. I have almost finished my closing statement, and I've been practicing it a few times to make sure I have it in my head. This trial is going to be long, and I have to meet with JJ, so I know what to expect.

"Hey, JJ," I said.

"Hey, how are you feeling?" JJ asked.

"Could be better, but I'm okay," I answered.

"I know it's very overwhelming, but I'll be sitting beside you the entire time, and remember, when his attorney asks any questions, only answer with yes or no, unless asked to explain," JJ explained.

"Got it. How does the court start?" I asked.

"You'll be called up to the stand. The judge will tell you to repeat a few things, spell out your name, and say your age. That type of stuff," JJ explained.

"Will they bring up the fact I have a visa?" I asked.

"There's a chance his attorney will ask you very personal things," JJ said.

"Personal things?" I asked.

"Yes, they tend to try to throw the narrative in as if you *consented*," JJ said.

"How do they do that?" I asked.

"By twisting your words, they may try to say you were a flirt—things like that," JJ explained.

"That's awful," I said.

"I know, but do not be intimidated. They're gonna do that to spook you," JJ said.

"How will I know what to say?" I asked.

"You'll know, I promise. Have you finished your closing statement?" JJ asked.

"Almost," I answered.

"Remember that the closing statement is the most important component of this trial. It'll help shape the jury's perspective," JJ said.

"So, there will be a jury?" I asked.

"Yes. That's the best way," JJ said.

"How so?" I asked.

"Well, Marcus has many friends in law. There is a small chance the judge may know him. This is why a jury is important because they will be completely random people," JJ explained.

"Random people who decide if he goes to jail or not?" I asked.

"Yes, pretty much," JJ said.

"I hope it's not a bunch of men," I said.

"It shouldn't be. I requested a mixed jury of people," JJ said.

"Do you think they will believe me?" I asked.

"I believe so," JJ said.

"I really appreciate you, JJ. I don't think I could have done this without you and Brooklyn," I said.

"I am happy I can help. Cases like these are important to me," JJ said.

"Why?" I asked hesitantly.

"Well, I see cases like these happen often. The court is so quick to belittle the women and blame the victims. I hate how often that happens. I wish I could take on more cases like this, but, due to my firm, we focus on homicides and such, " JJ explained.

"I'm thankful you took on my case. I'm happy to have met you," I said.

"I'm happy I met you too, Veronica. Now let's win this case," JJ said with a smile.

Chapter Thirty-Eight

Dylan Spencer
Friday, November 18th, 6:30 p.m.

I won't be able to play tonight since I haven't gone to practice in the past two days. I even told my coach I had math tutoring, but you can't miss any practices if you want to play in the game that week. It sucks, but it is what it is. Tutoring wasn't even that bad. I feel like I understand the concepts of the class. It was fun. It was like a challenge that I was able to complete, and once I understood everything, it became fun. I bet I sound so nerdy, like Brooklyn. I take my test on Monday morning. So while court is happening, I'll be taking a math test. I'm more than certain I wasn't going to be allowed in the courtroom anyway. I'll just be supporting them from afar, I guess. My dad has been trying to cut all ties with Marcus since he got the news about everything. I guess that was my dad's final straw with him. I knew it was coming soon, but I didn't think it'd be this soon. I'm happy my dad is nothing like Marcus. It's proof that no matter how messed up Marcus is, it didn't rub off on my dad, and I'm thankful for that. Even the way Marcus treated Brooklyn made my dad upset. He said

Marcus pretty much cussed him out when he brought home my mom, and that sounds just like something he'd do.

I hear my phone ding, and it's a text from Detective Clark. "I have found out something pretty big, and you are going to want to hear this immediately," it reads. I responded back, telling him to meet me at my apartment building. About twenty minutes passed.

"What did you find out?" I asked.

"I found out something interesting. I was able to get into the sex trafficking database; it nearly took me all week. I was able to uncover a photograph of one of the women. So, once I got the name, I searched her up, and it said she was abducted about three years ago. This means she is about twenty-three now. Here is a photograph of her," Detective Clark explained.

I take a good look at the photograph, and I almost collapse to the ground. The face is familiar. Extremely familiar. It's Elaine, Marcus's wife.

"I'm guessing you recognize her?" Detective Clark asked.

"Her name is Elaine now, not Lauryn Scott," I said.

"You know her?" Detective Clark asked.

"Yes, she's been married to my grandfather for about three years now, Detective," I explained.

"It says here she vanished at her apartment complex. She had reported stalking and said people would follow her around in the grocery store. The authorities ignored her request to look into it, and eventually she was gone," Detective Clark said.

"Of course, they ignored her," I said.

"Where is she from?" I asked, shortly after.

"It says here she is from Los Angeles, California," Detective Clark answers.

"This is not good at all. This must mean she was forced to marry him," I said.

"Most likely," the detective answered.

"I have to tell her I know. Maybe I can help her," I said.

"Kid, don't do that. It's not a good idea," Detective Clark said.

"Why isn't it a good idea?" I asked.

"It's been three years since she's been under his influence for way too long. She most likely will stick by his side because she feels she has too. She is most likely brainwashed by him," Detective Clark explained.

"I can't just sit here and do nothing," I said.

"Let me do the job you hired me to do. Let me continue to find proof so we can go about this the right way. If you say something, it might scare her. She most likely works for them now," Detective Clark said.

"Why would she work for them?" I asked.

"That sense of loyalty. She will not turn on him because she doesn't believe that she is in danger," Detective Clark said.

"So, this whole time, she pretended she was in love with him?" I asked.

"Not sure. There's no telling what she is thinking right now. It may be good that he's away from her, but, Dylan, please do not say anything to her. It could be really dangerous," Detective Clark said.

"Dangerous?" I asked.

"Extremely, Dylan. She could be in contact with those traffickers herself and could tell them you know about them," Detective Clark said.

"So, I just do nothing," I sighed.

"Correct. I will let you know as soon as I find anything else," Detective Clark said.

It all made so much sense suddenly. I always wondered why he brought around such young women. It makes my skin crawl to even think about this whole thing. It sucks even more now that I can't do anything to help Elaine.

Chapter Thirty-Nine

Court
Monday, November 21st, 9:00 a.m.

"Please rise. The Court of the Second Judicial Circuit, Criminal Division, is now in session, with the Honorable Judge Kavanaugh presiding," said the bailiff.

"Everyone but the jury may be seated. Mr. Lewis, please swear in the jury," said Judge Kavanaugh.

"Please raise your right hand. Do you solemnly swear or affirm that you will truly listen to this case and render a true verdict and a fair sentence as to this defendant?" asked the bailiff.

"I do," said the jury.

"You may be seated," said the bailiff.

"Members of the jury, your duty today will be to determine whether the defendant is guilty or not guilty based only on the facts and evidence provided in this case. The prosecution must prove that a crime was committed and that the defendant is the person who committed the crime. However, if you are not satisfied with the defendant's guilt to that extent, then reasonable doubt exists, and the defendant must be found not guilty. Mr. Lewis, what is today's case?

"Your Honor, today's case is Veronica Álvarez versus Marcus Spencer in the case of sexual assault," said the bailiff.

"Is the prosecution ready?" said Judge Kavanaugh.

JJ stood and said, "Yes, Your Honor." JJ sat down.

"Is the defense ready?" said Judge Kavanaugh.

Marcus's attorney stood and said, "Yes, Your Honor."

Marcus's attorney took a seat.

Opening Statements

"Your Honor, members of the jury, my name is Jenifer Green, and my co-council and I are representing Veronica Álvarez in this case. We intend to prove that on the day of April 28, 2021, Marcus Spencer sexually assaulted Veronica Álvarez. Please find Marcus Spencer guilty of sexual assault. Thank you," said JJ.

"Your Honor, members of the jury, my name is Steven Anderson, and my co-council and I are representing Marcus Spencer in this case. We intend to prove that on the day of April 28, 2021, the sexual interaction between Marcus Spencer and Veronica Álvarez was consensual due to previous mutual flirtation. Please find Marcus Spencer not guilty of sexual assault. Thank you," says Marcus's attorney.

Direct Examination (Prosecution)

"Prosecution, you may call the plaintiff to the stand," Judge Kavanaugh said.

"Thank you, Your Honor. I call to the stand Veronica Álvarez," said JJ.

Veronica walked to the stand and sat.

"Will the plaintiff please stand to be sworn in by the bailiff," said Judge Kavanaugh.

Veronica stood.

Bailiff said to Veronica, "Please raise your right hand. Do you swear to tell the truth, the whole truth, and nothing but the truth?"

Veronica said, "I do," and sat.

Direct Examination Questions for Veronica

"Please state your name for the court," said JJ.

"Veronica Álvarez."

"While working for Marcus Spencer, what was the work environment like?" JJ asked.

"It was very demanding. The work environment was not a comfortable one. Marcus was often flirtatious and made uncomfortable remarks about my clothing and sexual desires that he had," Veronica explained.

"What remarks would Marcus make?" JJ asked.

"Marcus would say things like how short my dress was and how easily it would be to slip out of it," Veronica explained.

The defense attorney said, "Object your honor, leading."

The judge said, "Overruled."

"Veronica, can you tell the court what happened on April 28, 2021?" JJ asked.

"The night of April 28, 2021, I was asked to stay late and organize files. The office was empty that night. The office always closed at seven, and it was around nine. I had my back facing the door, and I was organizing files in the filing cabinet. I heard the door lock, and I turned around, and Marcus was standing there. He looked me up and down for a few seconds and didn't say anything. Then he walked up to me and started to touch my arm. He slid his hands down my body. He then made me walk with him to the black leather couch in his office. I sat far from him, but he pulled me closer to him. He began to kiss me, and

I tried to push him off, but he wouldn't stop. He then sexually assaulted me on that leather couch," Veronica explained.

"What happened after the assault?" JJ asked.

"Afterward, I just sat there still. Marcus put his pants back on and walked out of the office and didn't say anything," Veronica answered.

JJ said, "Thank you, Your Honor; no further questions."

"The defense may cross-examine the plaintiff," said Judge Kavanaugh.

The defense attorney said, "Thank you, Your Honor ."

"Veronica, how did you hear of the internship in the president's building?" asked the defense attorney.

"I knew of the internship from the website when I applied at Morrid," Veronica answered.

"What was your reasoning for applying to Morrid?" asked the defense attorney.

"Objection, Your Honor, relevancy," said JJ.

"I'm building a foundation, Your Honor," said the defense attorney.

"I'll allow it," said Judge Kavanaugh.

"I'm interested in law, and Morrid has a very good law internship due to Marcus being a lawyer and one of the country's best," Veronica answered.

"So do you admit you had developed an admiration for Marcus and wanted to impress him due to his legal background?" said the defense attorney.

"Objection, Your Honor, speculation," JJ argued.

"Objection sustained. Next question," said Judge Kavanaugh.

"You mentioned Marcus was often a flirt in the professional environment. Did you ever seek help from the office or report this?" asked the defense attorney.

"No, I couldn't; he is the president," Veronica attempted to answer.

"Yes or no answer," demanded the defense attorney.

"No," Veronica answered.

"After the alleged assault, why was the school not notified of this?" asked the defense attorney.

"I didn't know how to come forward. I figured no one would believe me," Veronica answered.

"If you were allegedly assaulted, wouldn't it make sense to report it?" asked the defense attorney.

" I didn't know how to report it," Veronica answered.

"But in the event of this happening, did you continue to work? Or did you quit because you could not handle the embarrassment of being intimate with your boss?" asked the defense attorney.

"I did quit because I couldn't handle being in the same room as him," answered Veronica.

"Did you have sex with your boss?" asked the defense attorney.

"Yes, but it was not consensual," Veronica stated.

"Did you tell Marcus to stop during intercourse?" asked the defense attorney.

"I didn't know how to. I was frozen in fear, and I couldn't move," said Veronica.

"Did you tell him to stop? Yes or no," repeated the defense attorney.

"No but," Veronica attempted to say.

"No further questions, Your Honor," said the defense attorney.

"You may step down, Veronica," said Judge Kavanaugh.

The Prosecution's Witness

"Prosecution, you may call your one witness," said Judge Kavanaugh.

"Thank you, Your Honor. I call to the stand, Doctor Laurier," said JJ.

Doctor Laurier walked to the stand and sat down.

"Will the witness please stand to be sworn in by the bailiff," said Judge Kavanaugh.

Doctor Laurier stood up.

Bailiff said to Doctor Laurier, "Please raise your right hand. Do you swear to tell the truth, the whole truth, and nothing but the truth?"

"I do," said Doctor Laurier. Doctor Laurier sits down.

"Please state your name to the court," said JJ.

"Doctor Stephanie Laurier," said Doctor Laurier.

"I would like to bring forward evidence #8978," JJ presents.

"Received. Continue," said Judge Kavanaugh.

"Doctor, can you tell the jury what this evidence is?" asked JJ.

"This evidence is the underwear belonging to Veronica Álvarez," answered Doctor Laurier.

"Can you explain what was found on this underwear?" asked JJ.

"On this underwear, there were 1.5 milliliters of semen found. Along with blood spotting," answered Doctor Laurier.

"Who's semen does this belong to?" asked JJ.

"After further examination, this semen was found to belong to Marcus Spencer," explained Doctor Laurier.

"You mentioned there was blood spotting?" asked JJ.

"Yes, about two milliliters of blood," answered Doctor Laurier.

"What does blood indicate after sexual intercourse?" asked JJ.

"Blood found after intercourse can indicate painful penetration of the vaginal opening, which can indicate non-consensual intercourse." Doctor Laurier explained.

"Thank you, Your Honor; no further questions," JJ said.

"The defense may cross-examine the witness," said Judge Kavanaugh.

"Doctor, can you tell the court your education records?" asked the defense attorney.

"I attended Yale University as an undergraduate. This is where I got my bachelor of science in biochemistry with a minor in forensics. I went on to medical school at Duke University, where I was able to achieve my doctorate in three and a half years instead of four. I worked closely with the Federal Bureau of Investigations on numerous cases for about a year and a half," explained Doctor Laurier.

"How long have you been employed at your current job?" asked the defense attorney.

"About three months now," answered Doctor Laurier.

"Is it your first time handling a case where semen was being tested?" asked the defense attorney.

"Yes, I previously had experience with homicides and—" Doctor Laurier attempted to say.

"So you are underqualified to handle a case of alleged assault?" said the defense attorney.

"I have more than enough qualifications," stated Doctor Laurier.

"But you said you only have experience with homicides. Do you have experience in sexual interaction lab work, yes or no?" asked the defense attorney.

"No, but I have studied under many professionals in this field," Doctor Laurier explained.

"Who did you study under in the Federal Bureau of Investigations?" asked the defense attorney.

"Supervisory Special Agent Davis" answered Doctor Laurier.

"Thank you, Your Honor. No further questions," said the defense attorney.

"You may step down, doctor," said Judge Kavanaugh.

Direct Examination (Defense)

"Defense, you may call the defendant," said Judge Kavanaugh.

"Thank you, Your Honor. I call to the stand Marcus Spencer," said the defense attorney. Marcus walked to the stand and sat down.

Judge Kavanaugh said to Marcus, "Will the defendant please stand to be sworn in by the bailiff."

The bailiff said to Marcus, "Please raise your right hand. Do you swear to tell the truth, the whole truth, and nothing but the truth?"

"I do," said Marcus. Marcus sat.

"Please state your name for the court," said the defense attorney.

"Marcus Spencer," Marcus stated.

"Marcus, when did you first meet Veronica?" asked the defense attorney.

"Her first day of the internship," answered Marcus.

"How would you describe her application?" asked the defense attorney.

"Her application was not the strongest, but based on her last name, I knew how important getting this would be to her in this country," Marcus said ignorantly.

"Objection, Your Honor, relevancy. What does her ethnic identification have to do with this?" JJ said with frustration.

"Objection sustained. The last answer is dismissed. Next question," said Judge Kavanaugh.

"Marcus, how was Veronica's behavior in the office?" asked the defense Attorney.

"She was certainly strong-minded, a bit ditsy at times with instructions and filing. A nice girl in the office, but not very reliable. A bit flirtatious at times," said Marcus.

"Veronica mentioned that you often flirted with her. Did Veronica ever present to be uncomfortable with these alleged remarks?" asked the defense attorney.

"No, Veronica often seemed flattered and would respond," said Marcus.

Veronica says to JJ, "He's lying."

"Objection, Your Honor, misleading and speculation," JJ argued.

"Objection sustained. The court will dismiss that question," said Judge Kavanaugh.

"How often did Veronica stay late?" asked the defense attorney.

"Many nights to make up for the work that had not been finished during the workday," Marcus said.

"Can you explain to the court what happened the night of April 28, 2021—the best you can recall?" asked the defense attorney.

"Yes, I had returned to work later that night because I had forgotten a document that I needed to fax early that morning. I walked into my office, and Veronica was standing there organizing files. When I entered, she smiled and put the files down. We began to kiss passionately. I told her I was happily married, and this could only happen once and not again. Afterward, Veronica was upset because I told her this could not happen again, and she would not be able to receive any preferential treatment," explained Marcus.

Veronica says to JJ, "JJ, that didn't happen at all; he's making it up."

"So can you confirm this was consensual? Did Veronica ever seem uncomfortable or scared?" asked the defense attorney.

"It was completely consensual. It may have been unprofessional, but I made it clear to her it wouldn't continue," said Marcus.

"Thank you, Your Honor. No further questions," said the defense attorney.

"The prosecution may cross-examine the defendant," said Judge Kavanaugh.

"You mentioned you had a wife. How old is your wife, Marcus?" JJ asked.

"Objection, Your Honor, relevance," said the defense attorney.

"I'm building a foundation, Your Honor," JJ defends.

"I'll allow it. Continue," said Judge Kavanaugh.

"How old was your wife when you met her, Marcus?" JJ asked again.

"I don't recall," Marcus answered.

"It says here in evidence #6178 that you and your wife have been married for three years." JJ presented.

"I don't see what my wife's age has to do with this case," Marcus said impatiently.

"How old was your wife when you first met her?" JJ asked.

"Objection, Your Honor, relevance," shouted the defense attorney.

"I'm trying to build a foundation, Your Honor," JJ responded.

"Get on with it, please," said Judge Kavanaugh.

"So I'll ask again. Marcus, how old was your wife?" asked JJ.

"She was in her twenties," Marcus answered.

"She was exactly twenty, so would you say you have attraction to younger women, considering you are a man in his late fifties?" JJ asked.

Marcus does not respond.

"Thought so. Marcus, you mentioned Veronica was allegedly 'flirtatious;' shouldn't you, as a supervisor, have shut down those alleged flirtations?" JJ asked.

"I suppose. I was flattered. She looked up to me, so I was willing to let it slide," Marcus answered.

"Her role model admiration was one of the reasons you preyed on her. You knew she was vulnerable and had dreams of becoming a lawyer," JJ stated.

"Objection, Your Honor, speculation," said the defense attorney.

"Objection sustained; the court will dismiss that question," said Judge Kavanaugh.

"You mentioned preferential treatment; why would Veronica request this if she got the internship on her own? Did you read her transcript when looking at her application?" JJ explained.

"Yes, I did. A very smart girl," said Marcus.

"If Veronica is excelling without your help, why would she need preferential treatment?" JJ asked.

"I was wondering the same thing; she had much potential," said Marcus.

"Do you flirt with all the women in the office?" JJ asked.

"No, I do not," Marcus said.

"So, you just admitted that you only flirted with Veronica, and it was not her doing?" JJ explained.

"What? I didn't mean that," said Marcus.

"Thank you, Your Honor. No further questions," JJ said.

"You may step down. Both the prosecution and the defense have now rested their cases. The attorneys will now present their final arguments. Prosecution, you may begin," said Judge Kavanaugh.

"Thank you, Your Honor. Members of the jury, today you have heard testimony about the sexual assault that happened on April 28, 2021. I would like to remind you of some important information that you should consider in your decision. These facts include DNA evidence that proves the semen belongs to Marcus Spencer and blood spotting that indicates forced penetration. The defendant has contradicted many points and kept an inconsistent story; the defendant has a prior history of attraction to younger women, his wife, for example, the defendant willingly admitted to being flirtatious with the plaintiff. Please find the defendant, Marcus Spencer, guilty of sexual assault. Thank you," said JJ.

"Defense, you may proceed with your closing argument," said Judge Kavanaugh.

"Thank you, Your Honor. Members of the jury, today you have heard testimony about the alleged assault on April 28, 2021. I would like to remind you of some important information that you should consider in your decision. These facts include that the DNA expert is not experienced in this manner, and the evidence could be falsely presented. This DNA evidence was processed alarmingly fast. Veronica never made the office aware of her concerns. Veronica did not report the assault until a year later. This interaction was consensual and between two consenting adults. Please find the defendant,

Marcus Spencer, a lawyer for over thirty years, not guilty of sexual assault. Thank you," said the defense attorney.

"The plaintiff may come to the stand to give the final and closing statement," said Judge Kavanaugh.

Veronica walked up to stand and took a seat.

"Growing up as women, we are taught not to dress and act a certain way. When assaults happen toward women, people completely disregard the assault and ask, "What was she wearing? What was she drinking?" In this society, sexual assault is inevitable. Despite the various precautions taken, many still fall victim to this issue, such as myself. Specifically, college campuses are the areas with the highest numbers of assaults. No one should have their life ripped from them due to the vile and malicious acts of another. I am a victim of sexual assault. My innocence and parts of myself were ripped away from me due to the acts of Marcus Spencer. Women should not be silenced and should feel safe when coming forward with these incidents. I pray that anyone in this courtroom who is a victim of sexual assault knows that your voice matters, no matter what anyone tells you. I believe you, and I stand with you," Veronica said to the courtroom.

Jury Instructions

"Members of the jury, you have heard all the testimony concerning this case. It is now up to you to determine the facts. You, and you alone, are the judges of the facts. Once you decide what facts the evidence proves," explained Judge Kavanaugh.

"In just a moment, the bailiff will take you to the jury room to consider your verdict. One of the first things you will want to do is select a foreperson. It will be the foreperson's duty to sign the verdict form when you have agreed on a verdict. Whatever verdict you render must be unanimous, which means that each and every person must agree on the same verdict. The bailiff will now escort you to the deliberation room," said Judge Kavanaugh.

"All rise," announces the bailiff.

Veronica turned to see her family in the back and whispered, "My family is here, JJ."

"It was all Brooklyn's idea. She figured you needed some extra support today," JJ whispered back.

20 minutes later...

"Have you reached a verdict?" asked Judge Kavanaugh.

"We have, Your Honor," said the jury foreperson.

"What do you say?" asked Judge Kavanaugh.

"We, the jury, in the case of Veronica Álvarez versus Marcus Spencer, find the defendant guilty of the charge of sexual assault, and he will be sentenced to five years without chances of parole. His name will go into the Registered National Sex Offender Database, and this case will be reopened when deciding for probation after the five-year sentence," said the jury foreperson.

"Thank you, jury, for your service today. The court is adjourned," said Judge Kavanaugh.

"JJ, we did it," said Veronica as she broke down into tears.

"Yes, yes, we did it," said JJ as she hugged Veronica.

Chapter Forty

Dylan Spencer
Monday, November 21st, 11:00 a.m.

It took me over two hours to finish that exam. I hadn't been that nervous since we played against Georgia. I had been waiting for more information from the detective and to hear from Brooklyn about how court went. Those two things were racing around my mind the entire time I sat in a classroom answering questions about correlation and regression. My professor graded the exam right in front of me. Seeing him use his bright blue pen to cross out questions from right to wrong gave me so much anxiety. Luckily, I got a B-, so my average in the class is a B-, which is all I needed to be able to continue playing for the season. That was all I wanted. I still don't know what the future holds for me here. I love football; I always have. I've been playing it since primary school, but it keeps feeling like a part of myself is missing. I'm waiting for all the pieces of the puzzle to fit together, but they keep being the wrong pieces.

All the guys on the team make football their whole lives, and I get that, but it seems so boring to me. I just want more for myself. Mostly, I just want to prove Marcus wrong. He always thought I couldn't become anything great, as if everything I got were handed to me when it wasn't.

My freshman year of high school was when the competitiveness started. My dad was an athlete. He played every sport you could think of, like baseball, soccer, basketball, and even football. He was a "sports god," I used to say. If we still lived in the house in Pennsylvania, the guest house would be filled with trophies, medals, and awards he won. My father never pursued a career in athletics, though; he wanted to be a doctor, a neurosurgeon. I guess that's why he immediately liked Brooklyn when she said she wanted to be a doctor too. He was telling her about his practice here in New York City and about internships he had ready for her if she wanted to go that path. It made me happy because I could tell he believed in her, and she never really got that from her dad. I always thought my dad was cold; he was pretty unempathetic most of my life. He didn't show much care for anything, and he always had his guard up. I guess that makes sense when you think of who his father is. I always hated that because it felt like I never got that bond I wanted with my dad. But we were still close enough, despite this. I considered him a best friend in a way because of how similar he and I were. I mean, sure, he supported me, went to the games, and took me to football camps every summer, but I wish he had stopped the abuse sooner. I guess it feels bad to say I hate him for that. Maybe it was suffocating for him to see the same things happening to his son that once happened to him. It's called PTSD, or post-traumatic stress disorder. I always overlooked that about him, but the signs had always been there. He's jumpy around Marcus and won't be around him for too long. I guess he stayed close because he thought that's what Nana would have wanted, but I think he finds peace in knowing who his father really is now.

Chapter Forty-One

The battle was won. The look on Veronica's face is something I will never forget. There wasn't a dry eye in sight. Most importantly, her family came. I knew that seeing Marcus again was hard for her. On the stand, her words trembled, and she was scared. Seeing how malicious he was on that stand, claiming "she wanted" to be assaulted, made me sick to my stomach. I couldn't understand it. I don't get it. It made me so angry, to see that smug look on his face. He really believed he was going to win this case, and what sucks the most is that guys like him sometimes win these. The oversexualization of women has got to be the most triggering thing to leave a man's mouth. I never forgot what Dylan told me a few days ago about becoming a lawyer. It's been on my mind since then. Seeing how everything played out and seeing how determined JJ was to help Veronica made it all click for me. I could see myself doing something like that. Truth be told, I always thought I had to be a doctor; it's what I thought I needed to be. But it's not necessarily what

I want to be. It always felt like someone else's dream rather than my own.

I took a deep breath. Veronica was in the hall, talking with her family. I glanced toward her, and I saw that sparkle in her dark brown eyes, almost like she had gained a part of herself back today. She's tightly hugging her mom. She looks up at me and smiles, mouthing, "Thank you." I smile back and mouth, "You're welcome." I figured she needed this time with her family, so I walked out of the courthouse to the city. Today was a colder day. It was rainy; the clouds were dark, and it was windy. I cinched up my brown trench coat that Mariah got me last Christmas. It was way too expensive for me to own, but she insisted I wear it whenever I need a hug from her, and she wasn't here to give it. It was warm and expensive, just like her.

I reached into my clutch purse to get my phone. I needed to call Dylan to find out about his exam and tell him the good news.

Brooklyn: Hey Dyl? How'd your exam go?

Dylan: I got a B minus, thankfully.

Brooklyn: That's amazing. So, you can play now?

Dylan: Yeah, the guys are gonna be psyched.

Brooklyn: I bet they are. Are you?

Dylan: I guess. Enough about me, though. How was the trial? Please tell me that he's gonna be locked away.

Brooklyn: He sure is. Marcus was found guilty of sexual assault and sentenced to five years.

Dylan: Needs to be way longer for what he did.

Brooklyn: Agreed. I'm just happy that Veronica got her justice.

Dylan: I'm happy for her. And I'm proud of you.

Brooklyn: Proud of me?

Dylan: Hell yeah. You were the perfect person to be by her side. She had you and JJ. She was in good hands.

Brooklyn: It was all JJ, honestly. She made sure we went to court as soon as possible.

Dylan: Yeah, but Veronica couldn't have done that without your emotional support. You read the letter. She was scared to even go out in public. You made her feel safe again.

Brooklyn: I'm happy to have helped. She deserves the world.

Dylan: I love that about you, Brookie.

Brooklyn: Which thing?

Dylan: Your heart, your love for others. It's unlike anything I've ever seen in someone. I love you.

Brooklyn: You've got me tearing up outside this courthouse. I love you so much.

Dylan: Wipe those tears, beautiful. When are you going home?

Brooklyn: My flight leaves at three. I'm headed to my apartment to get my suitcase and stuff.

Dylan: Let me come with you.

Brooklyn: You don't want to spend Thanksgiving with your family?

Dylan: I have for twenty-one years. Let me come with you, please.

Brooklyn: What about Evie? She's gonna want to see you. Your mom and dad too.

Dylan: We've got a beach house in Florida. I hate it there, but you'll make it better. Come on, what do you think?

Brooklyn: Are you sure they'd be okay with that?

Dylan: Yes. They love you, and they love the South for some odd reason. It's utterly mediocre compared to the North.

Brooklyn: Hey! Don't hate on the South.

Dylan: The accents are strong there. I like your accent, though. So, it's official that we're combining our Thanksgivings?

Brooklyn: You're so stubborn.

Dylan: You love it. I'll pick you up soon.

Brooklyn: See you soon.

Chapter Forty-Two

Dylan Spencer
Thanksgiving Day, Thursday,
November 24th, 3:00 p.m.

It was officially my first Thanksgiving with Brooklyn and our families. I got to see Brooklyn's mom, Amira, again. Brooklyn looks just like her. They have the same skin tone, eyes, and hair color. I met her mother a while ago when she came to visit Brooklyn during the last spring semester. When I first met her, she looked at me and then at Brooklyn and hugged us both. Brooklyn said her mom never liked any of her boyfriends, and she never hugged any of them. I guess I was expecting her mom to have that traditional way of thinking, like dating outside your race mindset. I couldn't have been more wrong. Her mom welcomed me into the family immediately that day. To this day, she still wishes me luck at my games and keeps me in the loop about the things going on with Brooklyn. I also got to meet her brother, Myles, for the first time. He was a lot different from I had pictured him to be. He was tall, almost as tall as me. He was covered in artistic tattoos like music notes and such. Something about him felt similar to the way Brooklyn makes the environment feel—a feeling of calmness but hurt. I could tell he had a lot of things on his plate just by the way his eyes looked. But he and Brooklyn were alike in that way. You could tell they had so much heartbreak and hopelessness by solely looking into their eyes, but they didn't necessarily show it. They masked it with a smile that would make you smile too.

With Brooklyn, her smile always makes me smile. Like I said, I fell more in love with her as the days went on. I love her. I want to marry this girl—not now but one day. Maybe one day we'll have a beach house like this. It would be a big beach house right on the beach, so close you could walk out, and the backyard would be the beach and the ocean. She'd always wear her hair in her high ponytails, with some curls always escaping. We'd sit on the beach, and she'd be reading, and I'd just be watching her read. We'd be living our lives together, happy, and away from all the things holding us back. In the mornings, she'd be making her French toast recipe, singing along to all her favorite songs, and tasting the mixture before she was ready to cook it. She'd jump around with so much energy and joy, like she always does.

I'd take her all around the world. We'd travel to all the countries she wants to see, like France, Spain, and even Greece. Our life together would be peaceful and restful for her, and she would feel completely and utterly still and content. That is all I ever want her to feel because I know how overwhelmed and anxious she can feel at times. But I'd help her with that. I'd hold her hand and kiss her forehead whenever I could tell something was wrong. I love Brooklyn, and I will make sure she never forgets how much I do. No matter what happens to me.

Chapter Forty-Three

Brooklyn Reed
Thanksgiving Day, Thursday,
November 24th, 8:00 p.m.

Today was amazing. Our families together were perfect. My brother and Dylan's mom hit it off immediately. His mom is a music lover like my brother, which he never mentioned. The two got on the piano together and sang "Lean on Me" by Bill Withers together, with the rest of us singing along. In a way our families came together like we had known each other our whole lives. I loved getting to spend time with Evie. I didn't think she loved me as much as she did. But she clung to my side immediately and wanted to spend every second with me, which made me so happy. She was a lot like her brother. The glow in their eyes was enough to make a person forget all the bad things happening and just absolutely adore them. I took her to some of my favorite places here in Florida, like my old playground and my old ice cream spot, and I even showed her the old thrift doll shop. That doll shop seems a bit creepy now that I'm older, but she loved it. She told me she's turning six soon, and she's so excited for first grade next year. Evie's birthday is on Christmas day, so she said that she gets so many "extra, extra" presents. She told me she wanted a bunch of big kid toys; I'm not sure what type of toys she means, but I'm guessing she's not going to want to play with her Barbies.

It was dark outside, and everyone was winding down to relax. Evie was about to go to bed, and she was upstairs watching *SpongeBob*. Dylan's dad and my brother were in the living room watching "The Kardashians," and they made a huge fuss when Dylan's mom turned it on. Since then, they have watched a whole episode and started a new one. Our moms were in the kitchen, making margaritas. Our moms instantly became like best friends and have been inseparable for the past two days. I didn't think Dylan would have been able to convince his family to come to Florida as easily as he did. But he said they were drained from the press in the city and needed a getaway. I'm glad our families came together, though; it has been amazing to have everyone together.

Chapter Forty-Four

Dylan Spencer
Thanksgiving Day, Thursday,
November 24th, 10:00 p.m.

Thanksgiving was amazing, especially the food. This time, we had seafood. It was different because my family never did it that way before; we always went out somewhere. But I tried shrimp, crab, and oyster, and it was amazing. Evie even enjoyed it and had some crab, but my mom broke the legs open for her to get the meat out since Evie didn't know how. It was a good day. Everyone's in the house, but I came out for some air. Florida was different from I remembered. The air smelled like salt, and it wasn't terrible here. I knew I could like it here. The houses were by the beach and sort of close together. But I just sat on the front porch, looking out at all the houses. It was calm and ambient here, completely different from the busy city environment I had lived in my whole life. Brooklyn was used to this life, though, and it helped me learn more about why she loves Florida so much.

I was in my thoughts for minutes, until a dark shadow started moving toward the beach house. I got up to my feet almost instantly. I started to approach the shadow because, as she got closer, I recognized who it was. It was Elaine, Marcus's wife, or should I say *trafficked* wife? I immediately put my guard up and approached her slowly. She's standing there and looks shaken up, but she's keeping her composure pretty well, as I could tell. I take a deep breath.

"You can't be here, Elaine," I said.

"You know, don't you?" she asked. She paused for a second and then said, "Dylan, please be careful. You and your family are not safe in the city. They know that you know."

"Who knows?" I asked.

"I can't say, but, Dylan don't trust anyone except the people in that house. So many people are involved in this—so many. This is so much bigger than it seems," Elaine explained.

"What should I do then?" I asked.

"You stay away, and tell your family the same thing," Elaine said.

"I have to go back to school," I said.

"Your little sister and your mom need to stay here; they cannot go back with you," she said.

I took a second to come up with a response. Two of the most important people in my life were in danger too? I couldn't form words together because I was so confused about everything coming out of her mouth, and my mind was filled with so many questions. Why was Elaine here? How did she know I was here?

"Dylan," she said.

I look at her and ask, "What are you going to do? Are you in danger too?"

"I'm getting the hell out of here. I can't stay here. I just came here to tell you this," Elaine explained.

"Where are you gonna go?" I asked.

"Far, far away. You stay safe and do not trust anyone, Dylan," said Elaine.

She walked away and slowly disappeared into the darkness of the night. I quickly went inside to the guest bedroom. Brooklyn was already asleep with her beats on, most likely listening to music to help her sleep. I grabbed my phone off the nightstand and unplugged it from my charger. I texted Detective Clark, "I just saw Elaine in Florida. She knows I know about everything and says she's leaving for good. Should I be worried?."

Chapter Forty-Five

Brooklyn Reed
Saturday, November 26th, 5:00 p.m.

Dylan and I have been restless at the airport. Our connecting flight got delayed, so we had a layover in Virginia. I was pissed, to say the least. I don't have much patience at airports. I'm just happy we took carry-ons instead of checking our luggage in. I had just been sitting by the gate for the past few minutes, trying to check to see if my exam grades had been posted. I got an A minus on my biology exam and an A plus on my organic chemistry one, which surprised me the most because I wasn't expecting to score that high with anything to do with chemistry. I checked everything I could. I checked to see if I had any payments to make and if I had any work to do before Monday. Thankfully, nothing is due, and I can relax on Sunday.

Dylan walks to me with a bunch of things he's carrying in his hands. It looks like bags of foods from different places, things like Mexican food, pasta, Panera mac and cheese, my favorite, and even different soups. I take a deep breath because why does he have all this food, and who's going to eat all of it? Dylan puts everything on the table with a big smile. He sits down and begins to eat the queso and chips. He looks so pleased with himself that he's got so much food for us.

With a mouth full, he says, "You gonna eat the Panera mac and cheese? You love it, and I love you."

I let out a small laugh and started to eat the mac and cheese. "I love you, Dyl," I say back as I stuff my face with the food.

Chapter Forty-Six

Dylan Spencer
Sunday, November 27th, 11:00 a.m.

My mom and Evie stayed in Florida at the beach house. I convinced my mom to let Evie finish kindergarten in Florida instead of New York. My dad helped me, although he thinks the reasoning is to get away from the press, but it's way deeper than that. The press knows where we live in the city, and I couldn't risk someone affiliated with everything finding them home alone. My dad traveled mostly for work anyway, so I figured it was best. Plus, my mom now has Amira there if she needs anything. I even suggested that Amira should move into the beach house. Myles mostly traveled with his music, so he never stayed in one place too long. The three of them under one roof were good, and it will be easy to keep an eye on one another, just in case. I stayed the night with Brooklyn since Mariah doesn't get home till late tonight. We watched all the scary movies Brooklyn likes and ate popcorn. She loves scary movies, but I hate them. I spent the whole time hiding behind the covers.

She's making us some breakfast while I lay in bed. Don't get me wrong, I'd love to help her cook, but she's way better at it. The best I could do is scramble some eggs, which would end up being "too done."

"Dylan, come in here. Hurry!" Brooklyn shouted.

I jumped out of bed and to my feet. I sprinted into the kitchen, and Brooklyn was standing by the counter holding the remote. I see the news headlines, and I'm frozen. "Elaine Spencer, spouse of the newly accused Morrid University President, has been found deceased in her home. The cause of death is still unknown."

I couldn't move. Out of the corner of my eye, I see Brooklyn looking at me, almost heartbroken because she liked Elaine. Brooklyn doesn't understand how much deeper this is than just her being found dead. Elaine was in Florida on Thanksgiving, and she said she was never coming back. Why would her body be found in New York? Did she come back here anyway? I take a deep breath, and I walk to grab my phone to call my mom.

As I unlocked my phone, I received a message that said, "Do you see Dylan? Her blood is on your hands." I froze. Elaine told me not to trust anyone, no one but family. I hadn't told anyone about Elaine, and no one knew except the detective. But he couldn't be involved...Could he?

Chapter Forty-Seven

Brooklyn Reed
Monday, November 28th, 9:00 a.m.

woke up earlier than normal this morning. I couldn't really process that news about Elaine yesterday. It came on the New York news early Sunday morning, while I was cooking breakfast. Dylan seemed sad, but he was not surprised by this. I tried asking him how he felt and if he was okay, but he didn't seem to want to talk about it. I understand, but I can't help but feel like he hasn't told me all of it. I could be paranoid, or I could just be a worried girlfriend; it could go either way at this point. I have a gut feeling something is wrong. I know Dylan very well, better than he knows himself sometimes. I know his skin crawls whenever he sees bugs. Also, when anything has to do with Marcus, his voice shakes a little. Now, when he knows more than he's letting on, he will completely shut down and shrug things off as if it's no big deal.

I took a deep breath. I remember Dylan telling me Lucas was helping with his phone, solving where the messages came from, and all that. Ever since he told me about the German thing, I've been suspicious of Lucas. Come on—Lucas coincidentally speaks the same language as the language the three-word "code" was in? I don't like the odds of this whole thing. In all the movies I've watched with Dylan, the bad guy is always the person you least expect. A friend, a family member, a lover, or especially the well-known hacker. I'm always for giving someone the benefit of the doubt, but, God, I just have a feeling. I want to tell Dylan, but he's gonna want me to drop it and leave it alone. He's not gonna want me to worry about what he's dealing with. Well, it's too late. I had our friends immediately crossed off the list. Mariah can be a bit evil at times, but she's no mastermind; if anything, she'd be the handyman, the one carrying out the plans. Nonetheless, she wouldn't do something like that. She and Dylan disagree on a lot, but, in a way, they act like siblings, and I know they'd have each other's back no matter what. It's the same thing with Reese. Reese absolutely loves Dylan; they are brothers. Dylan would protect Reese with his whole being. And Reese would do the same.

Chapter Forty-Eight

Reese Woods
Monday, November 28th, 11:00 a.m.

The fashion line has been amazing, thanks to the woman herself, Miss Mariah. We were video calling the whole break, just sharing ideas. I drew a lot back home. Thanksgiving was never really a holiday I went crazy for. If anything, time away from my family was something I wanted way more of. Thanksgiving dinner goes two ways…the big discussion is politics, and the family has some big disagreements over something, then everyone just finishes eating in silence. Or someone mentions something about me being gay, and then it's a whole discussion. My dad's a pastor. My mom has her struggles with me being gay, but she never uses that as a dig at me. My dad's side of the family acts like him with the whole thing. They make it seem like being gay is a big deal. I just wish they would treat me how they used to. My grandma will say slick things about me being with a guy or make jokes. I was texting Nick the whole day, since it sucked more than normal.

November 24th, 1:45 p.m.
Reese: Every time I come home, I'm reminded
why I just don't want to be here.
Nick: What's going? You okay?
Reese: Yeah, my family just always has some-
thing to say. Whether it's about me being gay
or how I don't plan to do anything with my
life.
Nick: Did you tell them about that new thing
you and Mariah are doing?
Reese: They wouldn't care.
Nick: Well, I care. I'm proud of you, Reese.

That's all Nick had to say to make me completely okay
again. He's been treating me a lot better now. It's a sudden
change, but I'm not complaining about it. I had been wanting
him to change for some time now. We've gotten closer in the
last few weeks. He also told me Mariah talked to him that day.
Instantly, when he told me, it made it all make sense. Mariah
has that type of personality that can absolutely shake a person
to their core. She's firm and straight to the point. I didn't think
she would've gotten through to him, but she has a tendency to
say the right thing even if it comes across as mean.

Chapter Forty-Nine

Mariah Parker
Monday, November 28th, 1:00 p.m.

Like usual, I'm gracing the university with my presence. I decided it was about time for me to return. Everyone knows I tend to take my breaks pretty early. Yet my break was far from restful. I worked on some dresses and got into a few disagreements with my parents. They don't really understand why this is something I'd like to pursue, so they kept giving me the cold shoulder and their opinions when I just didn't ask for it.

They kept telling me things like, "You don't want to spend your energy doing something with school? What about after college? You're wasting all your money on fashion." It's comments like those that make me not want to tell them anything. It's suffocating. It's like they are trying to live through me and want me to live the life they imagined for me. I hate feeling like that, like my dreams are silly. I have plans; I do. They just don't know what my plans are for the future because I don't tell them anything, for that reason right there. I plan to stay here in the city and have a fashion line. I want to travel around the world to all the different countries and learn about their cultures and fashions.

"Mariah? Hello," Brooklyn said, almost yelling.

I took a deep breath and realized I had zoned out. We're all in the cafe: me, Brooklyn, Reese, and Dylan. I look around and they seem worried. I crack a smile, and I take my lipstick out of my bag.

"We were worried about you there; you seemed out of it," said Reese.

"What's on your mind?" asked Brooklyn.

"Oh, nothing; I was just thinking about some stuff with the fashion line," I explained, which was a lie. I wish I could talk about this stuff with my friends. They would understand; I know they would, but I don't want their pity. When people ask you, "Are you okay? I'm sorry about that." It just makes me feel helpless, and I hate feeling that way.

I got up from the table. "See you guys later," I said. I walk to my office, and I take a seat. I plop my head down to think about everything once again, but now I have a migraine. In walks Michael, and I'm so not in the mood to talk about anything.

"Hey, you," he said.

"Oh, you're here." I groaned, rolling my eyes.

"In the flesh. So, what are you up to?" he asked.

"What does it look like?" I said back sharply.

"You seem upset? Wanna talk about it?" he asked.

"No, I don't," I responded back harshly.

I can tell he's sincere, but I just can't deal with him right now. I open my Advil, and I take two. I continue to sew together this brown and white gown I have been working on for the past two days; it's pretty much done. I'd like to tell him about how I feel and how overwhelming this feeling is sometimes, but it's like I can't talk about it. My throat gets choked up, and my eyes start to water. I just keep it to myself. I mean, does he care anyway?

Chapter Fifty

Dylan Spencer
Tuesday, November 29th, 8:00 p.m.

've been rereading that message since yesterday. I couldn't stop thinking about how Detective Clark was the only person I told about Elaine's plan to run away. It was eating me up inside. Did I do this? Did I sign away her death sentence? So many questions with no answers. I took deep breath after deep breath. I needed to dig deeper into who Detective Clark was; who was he anyway?

I searched up "Detective Clark." I kept looking through his profile under PIs. I looked for what seemed like hours. By the time I got out of my own head, it was dark out. I almost gave up, until I saw a familiar face on the internet that looked like the detective, except it was a different name. The name was Jason Ross. In the picture he looks younger and skinner, so it was hard to recognize at first. There's an article listed with a title that reads "Twenty-year-old Jason Ross from Colorado is officially dismissed from the police academy."

On January 4th, 1994, twenty-year-old Jason Ross was officially dismissed from the police academy. Ross thought he had his whole life figured out. He was accepted into the academy after the death of his father, Robert Ross, who was murdered in his home. Ross excelled the first few weeks in the academy and caught the attention of many different superiors. Toward the end of his training, he was sent for mental evaluation after he struck his superior and attacked multiple trainees. Ross was deemed mentally unstable and unable to continue due to his violent behavior and outbursts. He has been placed in front of the board and has been recommended to attend a facility but has declined.

I was confused because most private investigators were police. I assumed he was a former officer—a stable one, at least. It seems he didn't even get to the point of earning his badge. This worries me because is he even qualified to be a PI? Was he even a PI? I needed to tell Brooklyn everything now.

Brooklyn: Dylan? I've called you twice. Are you okay?

Dylan: Brooke.

Brooklyn: What's going on?

Dylan: I need to talk to you.

Brooklyn: What's going on?

I took a deep breath. Where was I supposed to start? Was Elaine's death not just a tragedy but potentially a homicide? Or about the PI I hired, who most likely isn't even a PI, or a legal one?

Brooklyn: You there?

Dylan: Elaine's death wasn't a coincidence. It was my fault.

Brooklyn: How?

Dylan: She came to Florida, to the beach house. She told me I needed to leave the city, and my family did too. So, that's why my sister and mom stayed back.

Brooklyn: You think she was murdered? Her body was found in New York.

Dylan: I know. I think she came back home to get her things. Then she was killed. I hired a PI to dig into Marcus's past, but he's not who he says he is.

Brooklyn: So he's a fake PI?

Dylan: Yeah. Are you mad?

Brooklyn: Why would I be mad, Dyl?

Dylan: Because I didn't tell you this the day her body was found.

Brooklyn: You thought you were protecting me; I can't be mad. I understand. I'm just happy you're telling me now. I've been meaning to tell you something.

Dylan: What do you need to tell me?

Brooklyn: I don't trust Lucas.

Dylan: You don't? He's been tracking where the unknown messages came from.

Brooklyn: I know, but listen. How would the language be in German, and, coincidentally, Lucas knows it? He's a hacker, Dyl.

Dylan: I don't know, Brooke. Do you think he would do this?

Brooklyn: I mean, I do remember he didn't fancy you too much.

Dylan: But would he really go to this extreme? Blackmailing? Murder?

Brooklyn: I'm not saying he's the muscle. I just think he's the brains.

Dylan: Should we confront him?

Brooklyn: Yeah, we should. How about tomorrow?

Dylan: Yeah.

Brooklyn: In the meantime, I think you should go to the police.

Dylan: And tell them what?

Brooklyn: Everything you just told me. Show them all the proof and everything; file a report. Do it tonight, even.

Dylan: Alright, you have a point. I'll go tonight.

Brooklyn: Be safe. I love you.

Dylan: I love you more.

I got out of my desk chair and closed my computer. I threw on my sneakers and ran to my car. I started my car and immediately reversed out of the campus lot. I drove for what seems like forever. I had to play some music that would calm me down, something soothing but nothing was working to calm me down. I wish Brooklyn had come. She keeps me still and relaxed. She always knows what to say in these moments. I wish I would have told her sooner. I wish I would have gone to the police sooner. It's just when these things happen, it surprises you, it doesn't feel real. You always imagine these things happening to someone else, so when it does happen to you, you feel stuck and scared. I was scared.

I was driving along the intersection about to head near the bay. I noticed a car following closely behind me. A gray sedan, I think. It had been behind me for a while. I tried to speed up in hopes to lose the car, but it just stayed close behind. I was approaching the bay and the car came beside me, nearly making me lose control and swerve into the bay area. I quickly slammed the brakes, almost crashing, a second away from it. I took a deep breath and tried to calm myself down.

I was shaking. I parked the car off to the side, and I got out of the car and looked around. The gray sedan was far ahead, driving quickly. I tried to see the license plate, but the distance was too great. Hyperventilating, I sat on the ground by my car. Someone just tried to kill me. I grabbed my phone and got a video sent with a message. It was a video of tonight, my car swerving. The text read, "Stop digging, no cops. We would hate to have to touch a curl on Brooklyn's head." I needed to call Brooklyn.

> Dylan: Where are you?
>
> Brooklyn: I'm in my room. Everything okay?
>
> Brooklyn: Dyl? Are you okay?
>
> Dylan: Someone just tried to kill me.
>
> Brooklyn: What? Where are you?
>
> Dylan: Near this bay. I parked off the side.
>
> Brooklyn: What happened exactly?
>
> Dylan: I was driving to the police station, the real one, not the one on campus. I was passing by campus and started to drive almost on the main bridge and a car, a gray sedan quickly drove by me almost hitting me. So I moved right to avoid a crash and realized how close I was to the edge.
>
> Brooklyn: Oh, Dylan. I'm coming to you now.
>
> Dylan: No Brookie, it's not safe.
>
> Brooklyn: I don't care. I am getting my keys now.

She was stubborn. Before I knew it, I saw her approach off to the side of the road. She jumped out of her car and sprinted over to me. She was wearing a big white Morrid University hoodie, grey sweatpants, and brown Uggs. I always remember every detail about her, down to what clothes she's wearing, and how she styled her hair. Tonight her hair was down, and it was wet. She squatted down to look at me.

"Just getting out of the shower huh?" I joked.

As I finished my joke, she slapped my arm. "Dylan, how can you joke now? Are you okay?" She said all in one breath. She looked at me for a second and paused. I know exactly what she's thinking and how she's feeling. She's scared to death right now. I pulled her softly into a tight hug, and I feel her tears pierce through my shirt all at once. I never wanted to scare her like this.

"I'm okay, Brookie. I'm not going anywhere?" I said.

"Do you promise?" she asked.

I pull from the hug, hold out my pinky, and said, "I pinky promise. We never break those."

Chapter Fifty-One

Brooklyn Reed
Wednesday, November 30th, 11:00 a.m.

I stayed the night with Dylan. I haven't left his side since last night. I'm worried—more like terrified. I don't want anything to happen to him. He's just lying on the couch, watching some cartoon shows. I can't take my eyes off him. He's just lying there, laughing. He almost died last night. I could've lost him forever. I don't know what I would have done. He looks up at me and walks over.

"Are you still thinking about last night?" he asked.

"I can't help it. I'm scared," I said.

"I know. I am too," he said.

Today is an important day. We need to confront Lucas about all the things we know—like how he was a big part of this whole thing. Lucas has a motive, potentially since it's no secret he isn't really fond of Dylan or his family.

As we walked into his office, there was a young woman standing by his desk. She was tall, skinny, and had brown hair that was slicked down into a bun. When the door opened, she turned and looked at Dylan and me.

"Do you have an appointment?" she asked, crossing her arms.

I crossed my arms and looked at her.

"They're fine. They are here to see me," said Lucas.

The woman nodded at him and walked past us out the door. I walked up to Lucas's desk, and I was about to let him have it until Dylan stopped me. He looked at me for a second, then walked up to Lucas.

"What are you up to?" Lucas asked.

"I should be asking you that. What the hell is your problem?" Dylan said, raising his voice.

"I don't know what you're talking about, Spencer," Lucas said.

Dylan grabbed Lucas, lifted him out of his chair, and shoved him against the wall. He lifted Lucas like he weighed nothing. Lucas was half the size of Dylan. I knew this could end badly. I could tell Lucas was caught off guard, and I needed to immediately de-escalate the situation.

"Lucas, please just tell us what's going on. We know you're up to something," I said calmly.

"Tell your boyfriend to put me down first," Lucas begged, out of breath.

"Put him down, Dylan," I demanded.

Dylan dropped him and walked to stand beside me.

"We need answers," said Dylan.

Lucas took a second to look at us both, and then he walked back to his desk and sat, not making eye contact with either of us. I looked at Dylan because I had a feeling that he was gonna hit him or something.

"Say something," I said, slightly raising my voice.

"I can explain it to you guys. I just did this for money," Lucas answered.

"Did what for money?" asked Dylan.

Lucas took a deep breath. "The phone I gave you. It's set to record at all times. The data on the phone—all your messages and phone calls—are recorded and wired to me," Lucas explained.

"Who has his information?" I asked.

"I don't know," Lucas said.

"So you just gave away all my information to some stranger, and you have no idea who the fuck they are?" Dylan said as he approached Lucas.

"I don't know, I swear. I just needed money," Lucas denied.

"Money for what, man? You screwed me over," Dylan yelled.

"Listen, I just got a call one day, okay? Some older man was asking about you. He told me if I do this stuff, I'll get money for tuition," Lucas explained.

"Do you remember who the person is?" I asked.

"I never met this person. All exchanges were via email or on the phone," Lucas said.

"So, you're the handyman for this sick freak that won't leave me alone?" Dylan said.

"Come on, Dylan. I didn't think it was that big a deal. I just thought it was someone who wanted information about your grandfather or something. I did everything you asked; I still tracked your phone," Lucas explained.

"Did you ever find out where the messages were coming from?" I asked.

"No. I'm still working on it. Guys, the messages pinged from all the way around the city. There's no telling who is doing this," Lucas answered.

"Oh, of course you've got nothing. I want my money back," Dylan argued.

"I'm sorry, Dylan. Just turn that phone off. I will get rid of all the information on it," Lucas said.

Dylan grabbed the phone out of his back pocket and threw it against the wall, missing Lucas's head by less than an inch.

"Now give me my actual phone," Dylan said to Lucas, to which Lucas dug in the drawer to give it to him. Dylan stormed out of the office and slammed the door, nearly shattering the glass doors.

"I don't get it, Lucas; why would you do this? Dylan has only been kind to you." I ask.

"I know, but I needed the money, and that was more important than friendship," Lucas explained.

I took a deep breath. I walked up to Lucas, and I took a seat in the chair across from him.

"I'm scared, okay? Do you understand that someone tried to kill him last night? I could've lost him forever, Lucas. I can't lose him. I need you to promise me you will still look into this stuff," I explained.

"I will work on it, Brooklyn. I never stopped working on it. I knew the guy was pretty sketchy when I sent over his data," said Lucas.

"Did you only have his phone?" I asked.

"Yes, he was supposed to bring me his computer the other day, but he never did," Lucas said.

"What did you find on the phone?" I asked.

"I traced it all back to the same IP addresses. There are multiple IP addresses," Lucas explained.

"What does that mean?" I asked.

"Each cellular, computer, or internet device has an IP address specifically linked to it; it's what makes a device unique because the IP address belongs specifically to the device only," Lucas explained.

"How does this help us, Lucas?" I asked with irritation.

"I cannot find the exact address of this person, but I can find what country, state, and city they are in," Lucas said.

"Okay, good, so where are they located?" I asked.

"That's the thing, Brooklyn. They are located in multiple places. Some IP addresses pinged all the way to South Asia. I don't know why," Lucas said.

"What? How?" I asked.

"I don't necessarily understand, either. I will keep working on it. I understand how dangerous this is," Lucas said.

"So, I take it you know about the trafficking and stuff?" I said.

"I do. I did see the data before I sent it. I apologized to the girl who was assaulted. I was wrong to give them that information. I didn't think they would release that to the public," Lucas explained.

"I don't understand that either. I mean, if this person is working with Marcus, why would they help send him to prison?" I said.

"Wait, what if that was the plan?" Lucas said.

"What do you mean?" I asked.

"What if they wanted him in prison?" Lucas answered.

"It's possible, but how would he be able to handle business from prison?" I asked.

"There may be people he knows there, like maybe they worked with him or the other people," Lucas said.

"Do you remember how that message was in German, in the student database?" I asked.

"Yes, I do. Why'd you ask?" Lucas asked.

"Was Germany a country that you traced with the IP addresses?" I asked.

"Yes. Wait. Are you thinking what I'm thinking?" Lucas asked.

"Maybe. Do you think this person gave us a clue by mistake?" I asked.

"But why would they do that? Why would they help us?" Lucas asked.

"I don't know. Do you think this could be a lot deeper than just this person stalking Dylan?" I asked.

"Yeah, one hundred percent. I think a lot of this has to do with Dylan's grandfather. I don't even think Dylan is their ideal target," Lucas explained.

"Do you think Marcus is?" I asked.

"Possibly. There's no telling how many people he's screwed over," Lucas said.

After I talked to Lucas for a bit, I had a new perspective on these people's motives. What if they are doing this specifically to get to Marcus? Why would they go through all the trouble of stalking and harassing Dylan if he has nothing to do with this? Would they do this to scare Marcus? Is Dylan even the ideal target here?

Chapter Fifty-Two

Reese Woods
Wednesday, November 30th, 1:00 p.m.

was enjoying my spa day when the door slammed abruptly. I got out of the bath and immediately sprinted to the kitchen to grab something to use as a weapon.

"Ew, man, put clothes on!" Dylan screamed, covering his eyes.

"EXCUSE ME," I said loudly. "You are the one who came home slamming doors like an idiot," I shouted, stomping my foot.

Dylan was covering his eyes now, like a kid. And he says I'm the dramatic one? Whatever. I rolled my eyes, walked back into my bathroom, and sat back in my bathtub. It feels like everyone has sort of been in their own world lately, almost like the group is split in half. You've got Mariah and I working together almost every day and night. Then you've got Dylan and Brooklyn hanging out, which is normal, but it's been more than normal lately. I just feel like tonight the gang has got to do something altogether. It's been too long; I miss everyone together.

Chapter Fifty-Three

Mariah Parker
Wednesday, November 30th, 1:30 p.m.

I had been in and out of the fashion design hall all week. I have an office here where I keep all my sketches and designs. They gave it to me in my sophomore year when I won the contest. It was pretty much the best thing that could've happened for me here. The fashion design department here isn't the best in the city. I'm still happy I picked this school; it's the only university that would let me take these classes without all the science and math requirements. Nonetheless, the past few weeks I had been working nonstop on some new designs, and I felt pretty much disconnected from the outside world, so I decided it was time to check my emails, and to my surprise, I saw an email that immediately caught my attention.

Subject: Paris Fashion Week Showcase
Date: November 28
To: Mariah Parker
From: Renée Céline Avril
Dear Mariah Parker,
I'm pleased to reach out and say how much the company loves the sketches you sent.

We would love to have these designs show-cased in our Fashion Week Showcase in early December. These designs were such a breath of fresh air from what we normally get here. The designs were fresh, tasteful, and classy, especially the brown and white gown. I'm beyond happy to formally invite you to come to Paris, France. We would like you to arrive between November 30 and December 1. All flight accommodations are paid for as well as hotel fees. The hotel check-in is December 1st at 5:00 p.m. Please join us and get your designs out into the fashion world! *Voyager en toute sécurité*!

Best,

Renée Céline Avril

I was speechless, almost unable to move out of my seat. I could barely contain my excitement. Reese must have submitted the finished designs to the showcase and didn't tell me.

1:35 p.m.

Mariah: You're so sneaky, hon!

Reese: What have I done now?

Mariah: You know! LOL!

Reese: No, ma'am. I actually haven't a clue.

Mariah: The designs?

Reese: Are so good, obviously! You did good sewing and stuff, too, I guess.

Mariah: Really?

Reese: Okay, you did an excellent job!

Mariah: You didn't submit the finished products to Paris Fashion Week?

Reese: Uh no. Are they accepting submissions?

Mariah: Wait, are you being serious?

Reese: Yes. I didn't even know they were having it this year.

Mariah: Okay. I'm confused.

Reese: What about it?

Mariah: I got an email saying they want our designs in the showcase.

Reese: WTF! That's sick! Are we going?

Mariah: Hell, yeah! I'm just confused.

Reese: Uh, who the hell cares? We're going to France.

Mariah: But how did we get in? They even saw the brown gown.

Reese: I dunno. I didn't send anything.

Mariah: I'm confused.

Reese: Well, who all knows where your office is? Has anyone been in there?

Mariah: I don't know; you're in there sometimes. Michael was in there two days ago...

Reese: OH! Do you think he'd do that?

Mariah: Go into MY office without my permission and send photographs to a fashion showcase. Absolutely.

Reese: Well, don't be mad; he seriously could have done us a big favor...

Mariah: I guess.

Reese: Don't be so hard on him. I know you're scared of trusting him, and your feelings are one hundred percent valid. Just don't push away a good guy because of the history with another.

Mariah: You're right. I'll thank him.

Reese: And maybe give him a smooch.

Mariah: Blocking you now, lol.

Reese: No, you're not. We should make plans with the group tonight; maybe go ice skating?

Mariah: We've got a flight to catch tonight... Should I just push it back to, like, around ten?

Reese: Yes, I'll tell Dylan; you tell Brooke.

Mariah: Gotcha.

Reese: Now go talk to tall and handsome. Good luck!

Would Michael really do this for me? Why would he after the way I treated him and shut him out of my life? He's always been so kind to me, but all I do is treat him like he's the one who broke my heart, when he isn't. I can't help it. It's like I can't stop myself. I think I just pushed him away because I knew I would fall for him. I'm scared.

The next thing I knew, I was at his apartment door, knocking. The door opened, and there Michael was. Reese was right—tall and handsome. He's wearing black shorts and a gray tank top; he looks like he just got done working out. He pauses and looks at me.

"Mariah?" he says. But I can't even say anything because I feel myself backtracking, trying to convince myself not to do this.

I take a deep breath. "Did you send my finished designs to the fashion showcase?" I asked quietly.

"I did. Are you mad?" he asked, looking at me.

I paused for a second, and before I could process what I was doing, I hugged him, holding on. He hesitated for a second and then embraced me in a hug.

"I will wait forever for you, even if it takes forever for you to be ready," he says quietly in my ear.

I can feel my heart racing. I break apart the hug and ask, "Why?"

"You don't realize how special you are, Mariah," he says.

"I've been so rude to you, Michael. I know I have," I say.

"I know, but I understand. Sometimes, when people are mean, there are deeper things going on for them. I knew it could go two ways. Either you truly hated me or you just weren't ready for anything," he explained.

"What if I am now?" I asked.

"Well, are you?" he asked back.

"I don't know. I think so? Maybe," I said, rambling.

He laughed. "You don't have to know now. Let's take it day by day, okay?" he responds.

I nod. He puts his hand on my cheek and looks into my eyes. I could feel my stomach spinning around like it was a carousel. I knew my heart was about to pop out of my chest. He smiled and kissed me. And I let him.

Chapter Fifty-Four

Dylan Spencer
Wednesday, November 30th, 7:30 p.m.

Tomorrow is December first. It's my favorite month, along with my favorite holiday. It was Reese's idea to go ice skating tonight. The last time we went, I didn't do so well. Brooklyn is good at it. What can't she do? I don't know, but I'm embarrassed since I fell three times so far. It's cold out, and everyone has on coats and scarves. Brooklyn has on a white scarf with a red sweater, some jeans, and her skates. She looks beautiful, like always. I was hesitant to come tonight, out in the open, in the plaza. There are hundreds of people out here with their families skating. It makes me wish I was able to be here with mine. Seeing the little kids with their parents and smiling from ear to ear. It was a bittersweet feeling. A part of me wishes my mom, Evie, my dad, and I were all out there like one big happy family. Instead, they're hundreds of miles away and have no idea how dangerous it could be if they were here.

"Hey, Blondie, tell Michael to hold onto you instead; he's about to take me down with him," Mariah shouted from a distance.

It was funny because she brought Michael along with her. I could have sworn last week she hated him or something. I'm happy to see them together. Michael is a good guy; he's kind and one of the few good guys here. Surprisingly I can say that about Nick now too. He's really grown into someone completely different now. I truly think Reese brings out the best in him.

"Are you trying to purposely fall?" Reese yelled at Nick.

"Come on; he's trying his best," said Brooklyn.

"By trying his best, do you mean completely falling?" Laughed Mariah.

"How am I doing now?" asked Michael.

"Not completely terrible," said Mariah.

I attempted to skate over to Brooklyn, who is now by the rails just looking around at the city lights. She's in her own world. She's a perfect representation of someone who's too pure for this world. She's fascinated by the smallest things in life, and I'm just fascinated by her. One winter, we went to Central Park. It started to snow. Brooklyn stopped walking to look up at the sky, and she stuck her tongue out. It was the cutest thing. At that moment, she looked back at me, and she had the biggest smile on her face. I knew, just then, that she had never seen snow before. She did grow up in the South, where it was always warm and rained every so often. So being able to be with her and see her experience something I was used to is something I'll never forget.

I was about to head back to the rink when I received a phone call from a number I didn't recognize.

Unknown: Hello, Dylan.

Dylan: Who's this?

Unknown: Your friend.

Dylan: All of my friends are here. So, who the hell are you?

Unknown: Guess?

Dylan: Who is this?

Unknown: Out in the open with all the people you love. We're here. You know why we're coming for you don't you?

Dylan: So, what's it to you?

Unknown: We're here.

Dylan: Leave me alone.

Unknown: You know, don't you?

Dylan: Know what?

Unknown: Who we are and what we want.

Dylan: I don't know anything.

Unknown: You know more than you think.

Just like that, the call dropped. I didn't know anything. I didn't know who I was on the phone with; I didn't recognize the voice. I knew it was a male voice, older, with a slight accent, but I couldn't fully comprehend the type of accent. How would I know who was tormenting me? If I knew, I would have confronted them already. Or did they mean I have met this person, or I know of this person?

I put my phone in my back pocket, and I looked around. I saw all the different faces and people around me. I can't help but notice a man in the distance. He's pale, tall, lean, has curly hair, and has a younger looking appearance, almost my age. I looked back to see if anyone noticed this man looking at us all. They were all just skating around, laughing. I looked back, and to my surprise, the man was gone. He completely disappeared.

I heard my phone chime. "Don't say I never gave you anything. Walk to where you saw me; check behind the parking meter." I looked back at Brooklyn, and she's occupied laughing with Mariah. I took a seat, took my skates off and put on my sneakers. I walked to the parking meter where the young guy was standing. I looked behind it, and there it was. The picture of Brooklyn and me with her face crossed out. I took a second, and I thought to myself, "Why would this guy give me this? Was he the one who took it? Why would he take it to give it back?"

Chapter Fifty-Five

Last night, Mariah and Reese left for Paris, France, to show their work in the fashion showcase. I'm so proud of them and everything they have accomplished. I'm just gonna miss them this week. I'm not sure how long the showcase is, but I'm guessing about a week or two. I'm staying at Dylan's place while they are gone. I just don't want to leave him alone. Today he had weights, so he's going to be gone with the guys until later tonight, which all worked out because I had plans with Veronica. She's finally returning to school, and we are going to start hanging out more. She's a grade below us, so she has to stay in the sophomore dorms. I met her outside at the campus garden, which is beautifully white in the wintertime now that the snow has fallen.

I see Veronica approach, and she's happy to see me. I hadn't seen her since her trial.

"So, what are we gonna do today?" I asked.

"I've been wanting to decorate for Christmas since I got to New York, but I never was able to. Do you want to do that with me?" Veronica asked.

"I would love to," I said.

We walked all around Manhattan into the different little shops, but there was one specifically that caught my eye. It's a place called Léle Boutique. It's a French store that has all these different decorations, not just Christmas ones. Mariah and I came in here our freshman year; it's where a lot of our apartment decorations came from. I had a nostalgic feeling. It reminds me of a time where we didn't have to worry about who was watching us. I miss that. I miss when my boyfriend wasn't scared because it makes me scared. He acts like everything is okay, but I know he's terrified.

Veronica and I headed to a restaurant nearby the campus. The food was amazing. I got a smoked shrimp pasta entree with a side of garlic seasoned broccoli, which is the same thing I always get here. Veronica got a steak with mashed potatoes and string beans. I learned that growing up, she didn't eat meat at all, not even bacon. She said she was always against the idea of eating animals or something. You wouldn't have been able to tell the way she ate her steak—all of it.

"So how have you been lately?" I asked.

"Better. I finally feel like I have some peace and comfort in knowing this whole process is over," she answered.

"I'm happy to hear you're feeling better. Do you know if you'll be able to go home soon?" I asked.

"I don't think I'll be able to. My family likes it here. They're thinking of trying to move here instead," she said.

"How do you feel about that?" I asked.

"I'm not sure. Cuba's home. It's always been home, so I can't imagine my childhood home not being there, you know?" she explained.

"I understand. Just remember, it's not the place that makes it home; it's the people. At least, that's what I think," I said.

"That makes sense. I guess I would feel better about my family being closer. I'd be able to see them more," she said.

"I get that. I hope it all works out for you," I said.

"Thanks; I appreciate that. Can you give Dylan my thanks also? I don't know what I would have done if he didn't believe me or didn't introduce us," she explained.

"I will tell him, I promise," I said.

"You got lucky, Brooklyn. You've got a really good guy. Those are hard to find," she explained.

"I know; I'm so lucky. I want to marry him one day," I said.

"Already?" she asked.

"Yes," I answered.

"You know for sure you'd want to be with him forever?" she asked.

"Yes, I'm sure. I don't think I could ever imagine myself marrying anyone else," I said.

"I don't even think I could see myself getting married," she said.

"Why?" I asked.

"I just don't think I'll ever be able to find a guy who truly loves me," she said.

"That's not true. The way life works is funny. Sometimes people enter our lives when we least expect it, at times where we need them the most," I explained.

"Is that how it happened for you?" she asked.

"Absolutely. I wasn't necessarily looking for Dylan. He sort of just appeared one day. But it was a hard day for me. A day I will never forget," I explained.

"What day was that?" she asked.

I took a deep breath. "It was the day I felt really defeated. It was orientation. I had just gotten my award letter back, and I didn't have nearly half the amount I needed to cover my tuition. I was panicking. I didn't know how I was going to be able to afford a school like Morrid. I had applied for a biology research stipend. I wasn't sure if I was going to get that," I explained.

"Is that the day you met him?" she asked.

"Yes, during orientation. I learned his mom was from Cuba, and he made me smile for the first time that day. There was something about him. You know there's always those people you can tell are genuine. He was one of those people. I felt it," I explained.

"All the years you've been with him, has he ever changed?" she asked.

"That's the thing; he's the same Dylan as before. He still looks at me the same way he did that day. He still treats me the same way. He takes me all around the city. He knows when I'm upset or mad. But most importantly, he loves me even on my worst days, or days when I'm not myself. And to me, that's what love is—when someone sticks beside you when you feel like you aren't worth loving. There were times in the beginning when I truly thought he'd leave me or get sick of me. That never happened," I explained.

"You've got me emotional over here. I am so happy you have him, Brooklyn," Veronica said.

"I'm happy I have him too. Just trust the process; things are moving so quietly that you never know what will happen next; just be patient," I said.

"I will be. I have just been focusing on what I want to do next, and I really thought I wanted to be a lawyer, but I don't think that's for me," Veronica explained.

"What path do you think you want to go down?" I asked.

"I want to be a victim advocate. As a victim of sexual assault myself, I feel like I want to help other victims like me," she explained.

"I think that's the perfect job for you, and you will be amazing at it," I said.

"Thank you; just promise me one thing," she said.

"Sure, what do I promise?" I asked.

"Promise me you'll pursue what your heart wants you to do. I know you love science and you still could do that, but I can tell you love helping people in the way that JJ does," she explained.

"I promise," I said.

She was right. I admired what JJ did and how she's helped so many people, including Veronica. I would want to do that. I think I should pursue that. If there's one thing I want to be known for, it's helping those who need me.

Chapter Fifty-Six

Dylan Spencer
Thursday, December 1st, 6:15 p.m.

I hadn't forgotten about the guy I saw last night. His face keeps showing up in my mind because I can't shake this feeling that something bad is going to happen. I reached out to the detective again, and I am meeting with him tomorrow afternoon to talk about everything. I can't tell Brooklyn about this. As much as I want to, I truly think I am protecting her by keeping this to myself. There's no telling how things will change if I keep her in the loop about these things. I dreaded not being honest with her, so I just told her that tomorrow I have football stuff all day. I love her too much for her to see all the things coming out of the dark.

I hadn't spoken on the phone to my mom or my sister since they stayed behind in Florida. For a few days, my mom has been sending me pictures of Evie at her new school. Apparently, the school she goes to in Florida doesn't require uniforms. She's used to having to wear uniforms or such prestigious outfits. I like how this school allows her to be a kid. It's not all work, all the time. She's only in kindergarten; she needs to experience the fun that comes along with being young. I decided that since I was thinking of them, it's time I give them a call and hear all about how much they are enjoying Florida.

Dylan: Hey, Mom.

Mom: Hey, Dylan. How are you doing?

Dylan: I've been doing pretty well; school is back up again until Christmas, so just counting down the days.

Mom: Oh, gotcha. Eve's been asking if she'll see you on her birthday.

Dylan: She will. I plan to fly there with Brooklyn sometime in mid-December.

Mom: Awesome! Amira and I have started walking in the parks in the evenings while Evie plays on the playground.

Dylan: That sounds great. How's she adjusting to her new school?

Mom: She loves it. She's made many friends.

Dylan: Already? That's amazing.

Mom: Yes. Apparently, she has a little boyfriend, as she claims.

Dylan: Tell her no boyfriends are allowed ever.

Mom: She's so silly.

Dylan: I mean it; tell her no boys.

Mom: Here, I'll put her on. Evie, come here. Dyl's on the phone.

Evie: Dylan! Hi!

Dylan: Hi, Evie bug; how are you?

Evie: I am good. I like a boy. Did Mom tell you?

Mom: Yes, I told him.

Dylan: No boys, Evie; you're only five.

Evie: I will be six soon.

Dylan: Oh, God.

Evie: Are you coming home?

Dylan: Yes, soon; I promise.

Mom: He's got school, Evie, so it won't be till Christmas.

Dylan: I miss you, guys.

Mom: We miss you too.

Dylan: Well, I'll let you guys go.

Mom: We will check in on you soon. Amira says hi.

Dylan: Hey, Amira. Okay, sounds good; bye Mom.

Mom: Bye! I love you!

Dylan: I love you too.

After getting off the phone with them, I realized how much I miss them. I started to get emotional, then I heard two loud knocks, and I knew exactly who was here. I walked to the door, opened it, and there were Michael and Nick standing there with a six pack and some controllers.

"Are you ready for boys' night?" asked Nick as he walked into my suite. Boys' night consisted of playing video games, drinking beer, and, I hate to admit it, but gossip. The guys don't really hang around any girls, so it's up to me to know all the drama because I'm always around Brooklyn and Mariah. Now those two always have the "juicy" details.

"So, Michael, did you ever hear back?" I asked.

"Yeah, guys; I got the approval to be in draft 2023," Michael said.

"That's awesome, man; you deserve it," I said, giving him a proud look.

Nick rolled his eyes and said, "So are you leaving us, big dawg?"

"I got to. Academically I could graduate in the spring. It would work out perfectly. You know, my biggest thing was just trying to graduate from college," Michael said.

"I know your parents are so proud. Aren't you the first to go to college?" I asked.

"Hell, yeah. My mom has been waiting for this. You know, since my brother passed, she's been worried about me every second of every day," Michael explained.

Michael's brother played football too. He was good all through high school. He won lots of awards and could've been great. His life just changed one day. He got involved with drugs, smoking, and hanging around the wrong crowd. He stopped playing football because he just couldn't anymore. One day, he was shot and killed. They still don't understand what happened; they didn't get any explanation. Michael thinks it's because of some drug stuff, like a drug deal gone wrong. Michael was in high school when it happened. He doesn't really talk about it much.

"So, you got any hopes of a team?" Nick asked.

"I don't even know, man. Just them giving me their approval of the draft is enough to make me happy," Michael answered.

"So, you're gonna be an NFL player with an English degree. That's a new one," Nick said.

"Oh, shut up, Nick; he can't help that he likes to read books and stuff," I say with a laugh.

"What would you do with an English degree anyway?" Nick asked.

"I don't know—a bunch of things. I could teach, maybe even be an editor. I don't know yet," Michael explained.

"Would you want to be a teacher?" I asked.

"I don't know, maybe? I'm not opposed to it, I guess," Michael said.

"You'd be a good teacher, if that's what you decided," I said.

"He'll be a hotshot NFL player too," Nick chimed in.

"What about you, Dyl? Are you in the draft?" Michael asked.

"I got the paperwork, and I filled it out late November. But I would've heard by now," I said.

"How do you feel about it?" Nick asked.

"I don't feel upset. I'm not even sure I want to play professionally." I shrugged.

"What?" Nick asked, standing up.

"Come on, man; remember freshman year?" Michael said.

During freshman year, the guys and I immediately bonded and said we'd all go pro one day together. We made a pact that we would be humbled, and we'd go through the process of sticking beside one another. We wouldn't be concerned with winning, but we'd do it because we had the love for the game. I still love the game; it's been a part of my life for years. I just think I would want to do something else instead.

"I just don't think I love it like I used to," I said.

"That's fair. People fall out of love with the game all the time," Michael said.

"It does surprise me with you, though, Dylan. You're like the best on the team," Nick said as he opened his second beer.

"Yeah, I honestly thought you'd be in the draft before I even was," Michael said.

"I guess the world is full of surprises," I said.

"Are you gonna play next season?" asked Nick.

"Not sure yet," I said.

"Have you told Brooklyn about all of this?" asked Michael.

"Nah, I haven't told her," I said.

"She's your biggest supporter. She'd be a good person for you to talk to about this," said Michael.

"I know; I love her for it. I just want to figure this football stuff out on my own," I said.

"That's fair. Michael, let's talk about you and Mariah," Nick said.

"Yeah, what's that all about?" I asked.

"We're taking it slow," Michael said.

"Dylan, honestly, they have that whole new love look. You and Brooklyn are like a married couple," Nick said with a laugh.

A married couple? I laughed. For a second, I thought about it. Marrying her. She makes me so happy, and I know I'd love her forever.

"Uh, he was kidding, Dylan; don't actually get married," Michael said with a laugh.

"I mean, I'm considering it," I said.

"You're considering getting married?" Nick said with a mouthful of popcorn.

"I mean, maybe? I just couldn't imagine my future with anyone else," I explained.

Chapter Fifty-Seven

Dylan Spencer
Friday, December 2nd, 12:00 p.m.

I loved the way the snow fell and how quickly the city was covered in snow, just hours after the first snowfall. I woke up early and headed to the gym. I was stressed out. I hadn't slept for days. Brooklyn was out cold by 11:00 p.m. I just laid there. Looking at the picture of us, my fingers traced around the corners, hoping my mind would put together a clue—an idea of how quickly my life changed. When it was light outside, I was relieved that I had made it through the night. The nights now feel so long. They sound so quiet. Usually, the city is always busy. You hear the honking or the sounds of nightlife. It hadn't felt quiet before. Maybe I was just in my own world, or maybe I just felt lost. I never felt lost. I always looked forward to each day. I was never scared about what was going to happen next. I never dreaded the next day that would come. I couldn't help but feel like things wouldn't get better. What if this was the way life is now? Living in the shadows, but scared of the dark and wishing the sun never had to set.

I sat in the same diner. The diner we met for the very first time. I felt my heart pounding out of my chest; I could've sworn the people in the diner could hear it. The heartbeat. Detective Clark came in. He was the same way I remember, except he shaved his goatee. I think I liked his appearance better with it. He took a seat. He didn't say a word. He had papers in his hands, all inside a black folder. He took a second to look around the diner. I could see how strategically he looked at each and every person in the diner. He seemed as if he was paying attention to the things they were wearing, their appearance, and the way they carried themselves. I noticed that because I do that too. After a minute passed, he opened the black folder with the papers in it.

"Do you trust me, Dylan?" he asked.

"I don't know, Jason Ross. Are you who you say you are?" I asked back.

He paused for a second. I knew at this moment it was either the best decision I could have made, letting him know I knew his real name, or it potentially gave away my leverage and put myself in a bad spot.

"Ah, I see you've had time to do some digging as well," he said with a smile.

"Are you even a PI?" I asked skeptically.

Immediately after I said it, he handed me a paper. A document that had his name on it. Jason Ross. I couldn't help but ask, "What are you giving me this for?"

He picked the paper up and held it beside his face. "Do you recognize the man in this photograph, Dylan?" he asked.

Was this some kind of joke? A sick way to teach me a lesson about snooping? I crossed my arms. I leaned back in the diner booth.

"Dylan, I'm a PI. A real one. Maybe one with a history that many can believe is concerning," he explained.

"Do you think I'm playing a part in what's happening to you?" he asked.

"You could be. I don't know who I can trust anymore," I said.

"I'm not in this out of spite. I chose to help you. I wouldn't do that if I was plotting against you. It would be a colossal waste of my time, Dylan," he said.

I roll my eyes. He's a dick. I thought to myself. "So, what did you find?" I asked.

"Before I tell you anything, we need to establish a bond of trust here. No matter what I tell you, a part of you is going to doubt me," he explained.

"I just don't know, man. Shit is messed up." I shrugged.

"Did anything else happen? Any new messages?" he asked.

"Two nights ago, I went to the plaza with my girlfriend and our friends. I got a call from some random guy saying that I knew who this person was taunting me. As I got off the phone, I looked up, and saw a man watching me from the shadows. He looked younger; he resembled me in a way. He was tall, and he had a head full of curly hair. I got a text that said, "Don't say I never gave you anything." I looked up and the guy was gone. I walked over to the parking meter that he was standing behind. There, I found the picture of Brooklyn and me. The one taken from my locker with her face crossed out. I don't know if that guy was trying to help or just piss me off," I explained.

"He may have been helping you. He stayed long enough to where you could recognize him" Detective said.

"Yeah, he was watching me," I said.

"He was either an assassin or your guardian angel, Dylan. If he truly wanted to hurt you or your friends, do you think he would've waited around long enough for you to be able to identify him, if need be?" he explained.

"I don't know," I answered.

"Think about this, Dylan. This man knew exactly where you were. He had the opportunity to do anything. Instead, he just stood there, cowardly," the detective said.

"Is this supposed to help me understand?" I asked.

"Dylan. This guy could have been there for two reasons. Either he wanted to hurt you and was just cowardly about it. Or he worked for them and tried to help you instead," the detective explained.

"But why? Why would he help me?" I asked.

"He could have felt bad. Or maybe he thinks you can help him in some way," he said.

Is this what my life has come to? Not knowing if I'll see the next day because people are hired to kill me? Me of all people. A football player, who sucks at statistics. A guy who just exists. What's so special about me? What do I have that they want? Why me? Then, for a second, it made sense. All of this leads back to Marcus and the man he was. Involved in all things that should have gotten him locked up a long time ago. He was involved in a great deal of money laundering and was actively involved in human trafficking. He was hated by more people than I could count. Is my potential death supposed to be retribution to the horrible things Marcus has done? What would that mean to him? Marcus, as far as I am concerned, has always hated me. I thought I was like gum under his shoe. He's treated me as such. But it doesn't make sense. They revealed the news about him going to court, getting the public involved. They gave us a clue in German. Then my mind started to move thousands of miles in only seconds, but I just had one question.

"Detective, do you think there are people who want me dead, but also people who want me to stay alive?" I asked.

"What do you mean?" he asked.

"What if my death is like a trade? They can't kill Marcus because he's in prison. So, my death would be like retribution for all the things he's done," I explained.

"I suppose it's possible, but why would the same people help you?" Detective asked.

"Maybe they worked for Marcus; they were in his circle? So, they think protecting me is something they have to do for him," I explained.

"That makes sense. There's a chance Marcus getting arrested and sent to prison was all part of the plan," the detective said.

"How would they have known he'd go to jail? As terrible as the system is, he could have potentially gotten away with his crimes," I said.

"That's true, but no one has tried to hurt you yet, right? It's just messages and calls?" the detective asked.

"No. On Monday night, they almost ran me off the road. A car was purposely trying to do so," I explained.

"Dylan," the detective said, his voice softer.

"Listen to me carefully," he began to say.

Chapter Fifty-Eight

Brooklyn Reed
Friday, December 2nd, 11:00 p.m.

I spent the day reading, writing, and sleeping. Before I knew it, it was dark out. I had fallen asleep. It was pitch black out. The rain came and went all day. Tonight, though, it poured hard. It was so loud. I could hear the winds pushing up against the windows. Earlier, I couldn't put down my book because I was nearly finished. I hated starting a book and having to stop. I went to bed, and I looked at the view. The window was blurry from the rain. But I could see the lights that illuminated the city. I walked into the bathroom. I reached for my inhaler. I always knew when it was going to happen—an asthma attack. It feels like my chest is tightening. My chest feels like it's crushing. I took a second to breathe. I felt a shift in everything. Everything felt wrong. Everything felt off. I couldn't shake the feeling. The feeling that something was wrong. I used my inhaler. I put it down, and I walked back to the bedroom. Dylan hadn't been back. He wasn't in the kitchen. The living room. Or beside me. I processed that he wasn't back yet. There was a loud knock at the door. It was firm. It was hard. I rose to my feet, and I walked to the door.

When I opened it, I saw two officers. One was white with a mustache; he had this look in his eyes. This looked like heartbreak, like he had bad news. The other officer was a woman. She was tall and skinny. She had auburn hair in a low ponytail, slicked back. She looked at the other officer. She has an emotionless face, different from the man. No one said a word. Why was it so silent? If they had something to tell me, why weren't they saying it?

"Is there a problem, officers?" I asked to break the silence.

"A black SUV was found on the Brooklyn Bridge. It's identified as belonging to Dylan Spencer," the female cop said.

"Well, it can't be his," I denied.

"Ma'am, we found his license, and the vehicle checks out to be in his name," the male cop added.

"Well, someone could have taken his car. The guys take it all the time," I said, trying to convince myself, like I didn't know what they were about to tell me.

"His driver side door was wide open, and we found what we believe to be a suicide note," the male cop said.

A suicide note? I think to myself, I know my boyfriend; I know my person. I know Dylan Spencer. He wouldn't do this. He wouldn't do this to me. He wouldn't do this to Evie or his mom, Alicia.

"He was supposed to be here. He was supposed to come home," I said as I felt myself breaking down. There was no telling if this was true. They didn't have proof.

"A shoe belonging to Dylan has been recovered from the East River as well."

Shit. Shit. Shit. My heart dropped to my feet. My head began to spin—faster and faster. My heart was pounding; it felt like it was going to explode. I couldn't move. I couldn't speak. I couldn't process it. Then, before I knew it, I fell to my knees. The first man to ever love me kindly, truly, and innocently was gone? It couldn't be. That wasn't supposed to happen to us. We were supposed to have more time. We needed more time. Every memory I have of Dylan started to play in my mind. The officers helped me up and sat me on the couch.

"Our condolences, ma'am," the male officer said.

Was that all? I thought. They just break news like this, then leave while I'm stuck here trying to pick up the pieces. I was shaking. Then it stopped. Everything stopped. I couldn't think.

Before I knew it, it was morning. It was so bright outside that it lit up the apartment. I was still in the same spot. I hadn't moved. I couldn't. If I got up and walked around, it would mean this was real and that it wasn't just one of those nightmares. Maybe I'd wake up, and he'd be lying beside me watching those cartoons he always watches. So, I moved. I laid down, and I turned on those cartoons. I could hear his laugh in my mind. His laugh.

I thought about this time last year when Dylan and I took a day off from classes. We drove to Long Island, New York. From Manhattan, it was about a one-hour and fifteen-minute drive. I had never been to Long Island before. When we got there, we saw all these big houses on the seaside. Dylan said it's called "The Hamptons." I saw how the houses were so huge compared to the little house I used to live in by the beach in Florida. We drove around for hours, looking at all the big houses. We passed this one house specifically that caught my eye. It had a gray exterior and a tennis court. A family was outside. I saw a little girl with her dad. She was running around the garden. She was ecstatic. I remember specifically wishing I had that growing up. I still had the best childhood. I'm not saying I'm not grateful for everything I had. I guess I just saw a little girl who had everything: a big home, a garden, a tennis court, and her dad.

I remember Dylan looking over at me and asking, "What's on your mind, Brooklyn?"

I looked at him, and he glanced at me for a second and then looked back at the road. I looked at him, smiled, and said "ice cream."

He laughed. This was funny because I'm lactose intolerant, so I'm not supposed to have ice cream, not if I can help it. Or I could have the kind that was made for lactose people, but I hated that kind. Dylan knows I hate that kind. So we went to some place called Benny's Ice Cream. It was this big place here. There were so many people. Just standing around eating their ice cream. I saw people pass by on bikes. It was a dream. Dylan and I walked in and saw the hundreds of different ice cream flavors. There was cookie dough, chocolate, cheesecake, and cotton candy. I could go on. Dylan always got cookies and cream. I always got cheesecake. He always claimed he hated cheesecake but always wanted some of mine. I liked just the plain cheesecake. It was good. It was probably the best ice cream I had in a while.

"You know, life like this seems almost perfect," I said.

"What kind of life?" Dylan asked.

"The rich life, the wealthy. They seem to have it all. They look so happy," I said.

"They look happy? Look over there by the white Range Rover," Dylan said as he pointed over there.

"Do you see that man over there, yelling at the lady and the child running around by himself?" Dylan asked.

"Yes, I see them," I answered.

"Does she look happy?" he asks.

"She looks miserable," I said, looking back at Dylan.

"She probably is. These people around us have more wealth than we could probably even imagine. Yet, they couldn't be more miserable than both of us," Dylan explained.

"You think so?" I ask.

"Absolutely. My family has so much money, but I'm still miserable. It's not the money that makes a person happy. They could have the whole world on a silver platter, but is that enough?" he explained.

He had a point. I grew up not having all the things some kids did, but I was still happy. Was I extremely rich? Did I ever have a yacht just sitting around? No, I didn't. Dylan grew up in mansions the size of ten of my little childhood homes. Dylan wasn't happy, though. I guess I let my mind convince me superficial things in life mattered. The things we wouldn't actually care about if we didn't have them. I could tell Dylan would have lost all the money in the world to be truly happy. Dylan smiled and laughed more than anyone I knew. Yet he had so many things surrounding him that could have turned him into such an awful person. But it didn't. He was kind, real, and special. He was unlike anyone I had ever met before. I adored him, and I didn't have Dylan anymore. He was gone. A part of me was too.

Chapter Fifty-Nine

Brooklyn Reed
Saturday, December 3rd, 12:30 p.m.

The silence in the suite was suffocating. It was so quiet, you could hear a pin drop. Suddenly, breaking the silence, I heard a soft and delicate knock. The type of knock meant that I knew whoever was behind that door was someone important to me or to Dylan. I sat up from the seat I had remained in for the past twelve hours. I open the door. When I opened the door, I was surprised to see that it was Elle. Elle had been my best friend since fourth grade. She was short and had the most beautiful eyelashes I had ever seen. But she had a smile that just reminded me of why she was my best friend. I know that sounds silly. There was a way for her to just provide me with so much comfort. It was like we were in fourth grade summer camp all over again.

"I just heard Brooke. Are you okay?"

I hugged her immediately, tightly. Which was new for us because we were never the friends that hugged. We'd always squirm or shove each other off and laugh. But she hugged me back without hesitation.

"How are you?" she asked. That question seemed so simple and easy to respond to, but I just couldn't form my words together. If I said it out loud, then it would be true. She walked in, and I closed the door behind her.

We walked to the kitchen, and she put her suitcase in the living room. She didn't say a word. She didn't have to. I knew what she was thinking. Elle had a way about her that just made sense to me. We both could understand the other person's emotions without even saying a word.

In high school, in our freshman year, we had algebra together. We hated that class. We made the most of it, though. We would spend that class just drawing or focusing on anything else. One day, we had a test. It was just one of those long, boring tests that took up the whole class period. I remember it like it was yesterday. Elle and I have this thing—we'd look at each other and just know exactly what the other person was thinking. All it took was one look. Our teacher caught onto this one day. He told us we couldn't look at each other at all anymore during a test. He thought we were helping each other by looking. We didn't, though. We could've. But we didn't.

I just knew she was worried. I could sense it. I didn't want her to be. She had come all this way. All the way from California. I didn't think she'd ever come to the city. I missed her. More than I wanted to admit. Sometimes I wish she got to meet Mariah. I know they'd hit it off immediately. They'd be best friends, for sure. Speaking of Mariah, I wonder if she heard, or if Reese heard. I was wondering how Elle heard.

"Brooke?" Elle called.

"Yeah?" I responded back, noticing she'd already done a walk around the place.

"Can we talk about how you're feeling? And don't lie to me either," she said, pointing at me.

I took a deep breath. "I've been better. It just doesn't really feel real yet," I explained.

"Well, I'm not going anywhere," she said, crossing her arms.

"What about school?" I asked.

"Who cares about school? You're my best friend," she said back without hesitation.

I looked at her deeply. "I wish you got to meet him," I said with tears filling my eyes.

"Did you see a body?" she asked.

"Well, no, but they found his shoes," I answered.

"Do you know what happened?" she asked.

"They found a suicide note in his car," I said, getting choked up again.

"I'm so sorry, Brooke. I can't even imagine how you're feeling," she started to say.

"Enough about me. How are you and TJ?" I asked, trying to take the attention away from me.

She rolled her eyes. "Don't deflect. We're good, but I'm here to talk about you," she said, and I could tell she meant it. She'd argue with me until I finally opened up about how I was truly doing.

"I guess I'm not okay. I sat on that couch for over ten hours, Elle. I don't know what I'm going to do. Knowing I can't hear him call me Brookie again. Or want to go on little trips around the city. Who's gonna calm me down before a test or presentation? He was another piece of me. He was everything I needed," I ranted. It was all true. I was grieving. Most importantly, I wanted to know how Elle knew. I hadn't told her. Quietly, I asked, "How did you know about what happened to him?"

"It was on the news last night. You haven't watched the news, have you?" she asked hesitantly.

I walked toward the couch, and I picked up the remote. I frantically turned on the TV. I took a seat. I changed to the news channel for the city. I felt my hands fidgeting with the remote. Then I saw it. His football picture was on the news. With the headline, "Morrid University Junior Athlete Dylan Spencer's black SUV found with suicide note." I turned up the TV. I could hear the reporter saying that there was a note, and only his family was able to read it. The police are at a standstill with everything because of the storm. Finding his body in the river was going to be nearly impossible because it led to the other bodies of water. There wasn't much they could do. His body was officially declared lost at sea. They said they were still searching, but I know that after a while they're going to stop looking. He was gone. I turned off the TV. I leaned back on the couch. I couldn't help but wonder what he was thinking before he jumped.

"Hey, I'm gonna run to the pharmacy. I'm low on my asthma medicine," I said to Elle.

"Okay, I'll come with you," she said, standing up.

"Don't," I said firmly. "I mean, I'm just gonna walk; it's down the street. I just want to be alone, Elle," I said. I didn't mean it. I don't like to be alone. I didn't mean to snap at her. I walked into his bedroom. It was messy, like it always had been. His favorite pair of gray sweatpants were lying on the bed. I picked them up, and I put them on. They were way too big, but it didn't matter. I found my Uggs and put them on too. I walked to his closet to find a hoodie. He had so many.

His red Nike one was his favorite, though, because red is his favorite color. The color he wore the most. So, I put that one on. I wiped my tears with the sleeve. It still smelled like him. The room did too. I took a deep breath, and I walked out to the living room to see Elle, who was on her computer. She's studying computer science and technology, so she's "computer smart," as I would always say. She wants to work for the FBI one day. She had put her furry black zip up on.

She looked up at me and said, "Promise me you'll be safe."

"I promise," I said.

When I got down to the lobby, it was quiet. I walked outside. It was freezing. I clutched my arms to my chest. I looked around to see the whiteness of the snow and how beautiful it was. I walked first to the pharmacy. It was about a ten minute walk from Dyl's. I walked in and got my prescription. I looked around the place, and I got some peanut M&Ms. It was our favorite. We'd always share them. I began to walk out of the pharmacy.

"Hey, where are you going?" the worker said, walking towards me.

Shit. I didn't pay. I turned around. "I'm sorry. I didn't realize I didn't pay," I said apologetically. I went to the counter and put the M&Ms on there. I paid. Apologized again. Then I left.

I walked again. It started to snow harder. The mix between rain and snow was confusing. Just last night, it was raining. Now it's snowing. I couldn't help but stop walking. Just to capture a picture in my mind of how beautiful everything looked. I wish I cherished our time together more. Maybe I took him for granted. Maybe I didn't appreciate him enough. I cracked my knuckles. I opened the M&Ms, and I put the pill bottle in the sweatpants pocket. I began to eat the M&Ms. But not the red ones. I know that sounds silly. I just always gave Dylan the red ones. So, I couldn't eat them. I took the long way back. I just wanted to walk around and be in my own head for a bit.

When I came back, Elle was sitting at the bar in the kitchen. When I came in, she got up immediately.

"Where have you been? I've been calling you," she said. There was concern in her voice, but mostly she was upset.

"I left my phone here," I said, shrugging my shoulders.

"Yeah, I know that now," Elle says.

I felt bad. But I didn't show it.

"Someone named Alicia was calling you a lot," she said as I walked toward the bedroom. I stopped. Alicia. Dylan's mom. I needed to talk to her. I just couldn't yet.

Chapter Sixty

Brooklyn Reed
Monday, December 5th, 10:00 a.m.

I woke up. I got out of bed. My phone was ringing. I picked it up off the nightstand. It's Alicia. I take a deep breath. I answer.

Alicia: I've been calling. Did you hear?

Brooklyn: Yeah. I found out Friday night.

Alicia: How are you?

Brooklyn: I should be asking you that.

Alicia: No. I need to know how you are.

Brooklyn: I'm upset.

Alicia: Me too.

Brooklyn: How's Evie?

Alicia: She's sad. She doesn't really understand.

Brooklyn: I can't even imagine how she feels.

Alicia: Tell me how you feel, Brooklyn.

Brooklyn: I can't put it into words. I feel empty.

Alicia: I can hear it in your voice.

Brooklyn: How do you sound so put together?

Alicia: Trust me. I'm not. I have to think strategically, once for Evie and then for Nathaniel.

Brooklyn: How did Nathaniel take the news?

Alicia: He's a basket case. He never really budges much with how he feels. He misses his son. He's been sitting by the beach every day, wanting to be alone.

Brooklyn: I'm sorry.

Alicia: Why are you sorry?

Brooklyn: Because I didn't answer sooner. I was just out of it.

Alicia: I understand. Everyone processes things differently.

Brooklyn: Are you coming back here?

Alicia: Eventually. For the funeral.

The funeral? It seemed that they already had it planned. I couldn't imagine it. I didn't want to. They found a note that he wrote, which said, "I'm sorry I had to do this. This was the only way."

"Had Dylan said anything to you about being depressed?" she asked.

But he hadn't. Dylan was the liveliest guy I knew. He wore his heart on his sleeve. Most importantly, he wouldn't leave his family behind at times like this. Not with everything that was going on. Then it all made sense to me. With everything going on, did he just snap? Lose his mind? Did I miss all the signs? I saw Dylan on Friday. He woke up. Gave me a kiss on the forehead. That was the last time I saw him.

After I got off the phone with Alicia, I just sat in the living room. Elle had gone out to get us Starbucks. I sat and opened Dylan's computer, since mine is back at my place. I went to his email to switch accounts to be able to log into mine. I noticed a string of unknown emails. Emails he never told me about. There's a video of me, but I didn't know that the video was being taken. I continued looking, and I realized he had been getting these emails for months. At first, they weren't too bad. It seemed like fan girls or girls who got his information. I had to think. I wasn't sure if Lucas knew about these messages or if he was able to track them. I forwarded all the emails to Lucas in a thread.

> *Forwarded Email*
> To: Lucas Carter
> From: Dylan Spencer
> Hey,
> This is Brooklyn. I know this is weird timing.
> Do you think you could trace these messages?
> I just can't help but shake the feeling that these
> messages might be important or give insight
> on what's going on. Please let me know if you
> can help.

I sent it. I closed the computer. Lucas was the only other person who knew as much as I did about this situation, and I wanted to hear his thoughts. Elle walked in, and she seemed sort of down, not like herself.

"You okay?" I asked.

"Yeah, I just got off the phone with TJ," she said slowly.

"Well, you don't seem too happy; are you?" I asked.

"I broke up with him," she said.

"Wait, why? I thought everything was going well," I asked.

"Well, it wasn't. He sort of sucked," she answered.

"You're not telling me something," I said.

She takes a deep breath. "Well, we've just been arguing a lot lately. He's always worried about what I'm doing and where I'm going. A few weeks ago, I walked away from him, and he yanked me by my arm," Elle explained.

"Oh my god," I said, holding my chest.

"You've been so upset lately, B. I just didn't want you to worry about me," she said.

"You know how important you are to me. I wish you would've told me when this was going on," I said.

"Yeah, it's just, I guess, I didn't know how to talk about it. I just loved him. I thought it was my fault when he'd get so mad and throw things," she explained.

"I'm happy you told me now. There's no way you're going back to him. And remember, it's never your fault," I said, crossing my arms.

"I don't have a choice," she says, taking a deep breath.

"Why?" I asked.

"I love him. We've been together since high school," she explained.

"That's no excuse, Elle. If he really loved you, do you think he'd treat you like that? There are so many guys out there. Guys who will appreciate you, love you, take care of you, and, most importantly, put your needs above their own," I explained.

"I'm just scared to let him go," she said, tearing up.

I take a deep breath. "If you accept his behavior, he's only going to get worse. You can't let him belittle you or treat you that way. Come on, if this was me, you know you'd tell me the same thing," I explained.

"Well, I did years ago," she said with a laugh.

"And I listened to you then," I said.

"After me telling you for months," she said, wiping her tears.

"Whatever, it was our high school days. I never listened to anyone," I said.

"Very true. Do you mind if I use the computer here to upload some files?" Elle asked.

"Go for it."

She took a seat where I was, and it reminded me that I forgot to log out. My mind filled with panic for a second.

"What's this email about?" she asked.

Shit. "It's nothing," I said, exiting the email tab.

"You're lying. What happened?" she asked, more aggressively this time.

So, I told her. I couldn't necessarily lie about it. She would have gotten the truth out of me eventually. I watched her face slowly grow more concerned after I started from the beginning and shared how things gradually escalated.

"So what does this Lucas guy do?" she asked.

"Well, he was selling Dylan's data to some random guy who was paying him by giving him money for his tuition," I explained.

"So, what the hell makes you think that you can trust this Lucas guy now?" she asked.

"I don't know. He did help Dylan, and he told us everything he knew," I answered.

"I don't like him. I need to meet him to decide," she said, crossing her arms.

Elle had a point. Could I really trust Lucas? He did play a part in things going completely wrong, especially with the information about the assault. Why would it be a good idea for me to trust him now? The truth is, he was all I had. He was the only person who would have been able to help. I wish I could have told Elle sooner. She was a better hacker, and she had knowledge Lucas didn't even understand at his level. I guessed maybe if they worked together. I just didn't want Elle involved. I knew how dangerous it was now that I knew everything.

"So do you think the Elaine woman was involved too?" she asked.

"I'm not sure. I think she was just a victim. I mean, she did warn Dylan before she was killed," I explained.

"Do you think maybe she was involved, and she just went against her 'orders' or something?" Elle said.

"There's a chance of that," I said.

"Call Lucas. I want to meet him," she said.

Chapter Sixty-One

Lucas Carter
Monday, December 5th, 4:45 p.m.

I was summoned to the Spencer suite via a phone call from Brooklyn Reed. It was almost unreal. A call from her wasn't likely, nor was an invitation to the suite, which was the nicest housing on campus. I walked from my office after closing the building for the semester. Since the semester was over, my job there was done too. I had mixed emotions about it, but it was for the best. I guess I should have used the money wisely. Now, my other source of tuition help is gone. I didn't know how to pick between what I had to do now and what I wanted to do now.

I stood outside the door and knocked. When the door opened, there was a woman standing there. She was petite, had short hair, and was pretty. I just looked for a second, and she crossed her arms.

"Can I help you?" she asked in a harsh tone.

"Elle, it's Lucas; let him in," I heard Brooklyn shout from inside the suite.

Elle moved out of the entrance and motioned for me to come in, and she shifted to a weary smile.

"So, what was so urgent?" I asked.

"I wanted to talk about Dylan," she said.

My eyes shifted to Elle. "Does she know?" I asked, looking at her.

She rolls her eyes. "Of course, I do," she said, crossing her arms.

I could sense that she must know my part in everything. "Ah, I see," I said. I knew my presence here was odd. After what I heard happened to Dylan, I knew Dylan wasn't my biggest fan. I still know how important he is to Brooklyn. I guess it's normal for her to be in some sort of denial about what happened to him. If it was someone I loved, I guess I would be too.

"Did you see my email?" Brooklyn asked impatiently.

"Yes, I did. Care to show me the computer?" I asked.

"It's right here," Elle said, looking at it on the kitchen counter.

I walked to the counter and took a seat at the kitchen island. I opened the computer, and I looked through his emails. They varied from brand deals, practice videos, and Amazon emails. I noticed that Brooklyn starred all the emails she wanted me to look at. There were over twenty emails from unknown addresses. Many were sent without a subject and were just images. The images varied from Dylan just walking around to a few of Brooklyn as well. I kept looking through his emails. It looked like I found a few fan emails.

"I also got a random email one day; here look." Brooklyn showed me her computer. It was an email with no subject and just an image. The image is of Dylan and Brooklyn, and they were sitting down in the lobby of a building. It looks as though it's a screenshot taken on a security camera.

"When was this taken?" I asked.

"It was the night Dylan told me about Veronica," she said.

Instantly, I felt regret. This was the girl who was assaulted by Marcus; I was the reason her information and case got out to the public. I noticed in the screenshot that Dylan wasn't holding his phone.

"Did Dylan and you ever text about this assault via text?" I asked.

"No, everything was communicated in person, and I only ever communicated with her," she explained.

I paused for a second. "I never sent any audio to the person. I just sent his text messages; you're telling me none of the assault discussions were on his phone?" I asked.

"No," Brooklyn answered.

So, it wasn't my fault. I didn't do this. I didn't release this information, and I'm not even sure how this information got out. I didn't say anything. I just nodded my head. I continued looking at the computer. "Do you have a notepad?" I asked.

"Yeah," Brooklyn said, and she came back and brought me one. I wrote down all the email addresses.

1. usernameunknown@gmail.com
2. unknownusername@gmail.com
3. username243125@gmail.com
4. unknown6889@gmail.com
5. 9532108u2819@gmail.com

These five emails were the most common. "I don't have my computer for my software" I said.

Elle walked up to the counter with her computer. "Here," she said as she placed it beside Dylan's computer.

I opened her computer, and I was amazed. She had all the software I could have dreamed of having. I tried to contain my enthusiasm for a computer in a purple case. I started to type again and again.

"Need some help?" Elle asked. I stopped to type. I wasn't used to anyone wanting to help or knowing how to.

"Yeah, sure, just send me the files from Dylan's computer," I said.

After a few minutes, I stopped typing.

"Why are you stopping?" Elle asked.

"It's not going anywhere. We aren't going to find anything," I said.

"Why the hell not?" Brooklyn asked, walking back into the kitchen.

I wasn't sure what to say back.

Hesitantly, I said, "The emails are gonna require a lot more than finding out where they came from."

Elle looked over at Brooklyn, almost like she knew how upset that made her. "Brooklyn, we tried," she said.

I looked over at Brooklyn, and she just stared at us. She's not saying anything.

"I just thought we could find something to help him in any way," Brooklyn said, breaking the silence.

"I'm sorry I couldn't do more," I apologized.

"I still don't understand how we can suddenly trust you now," Elle said, once again crossing her arms.

"I wouldn't have come here with ill intentions. I told you guys I was here to help," I said.

"Sure you are," Elle said, but I can sense her skepticism.

I understand they have no reason to trust me, and I'm a shitty guy because of the way I handled everything. It's just that when Dylan told me all about this, I didn't take it as seriously as I should have. Initially my plan was to help him. I didn't think the person I talked to had anything to do with what was happening to him. It was just a coincidence. I understand I shouldn't have helped this person, but I just needed the money. I still feel guilty. Maybe if I tried harder, Dylan would be here now.

Chapter Sixty-Two

Reese Woods
Monday, December 5th, 6:30 p.m.

I sat on the airplane anxiously, waiting for it to land. Ever since I got the news about Dylan, I have been a mess. I felt like, as his best friend, I should have noticed something was wrong. This all feels so twisted, sick, and unreal. It doesn't seem like something Dylan would do. Mariah and I had been in Paris for a few days. Our showcase doesn't finish until this week, but we loved Dylan. We wanted more than anything to be there for his family and Brooklyn. I can't even imagine how she's feeling right now. She and Dylan were always together, and they hardly ever left each other by themselves. They were the other halves of each other, and based on the email she sent us a few days ago, she doesn't seem to be doing too well.

> Subject: Dylan
> To: Reese Woods, Mariah Parker
> From: Brooklyn Reed
> Hey, guys,
> I know you're in Paris and so busy, but a lot
> has happened since you guys left. Friday night,

they found Dylan's black SUV abandoned on the Brooklyn Bridge. There was a note. They think he jumped into the river. They found his shoe, and they believe his body is lost. They are ruling it a suicide. I'm heartbroken; his mom is talking about how the police don't think they will find a body. I feel stuck. I miss him.

Love you guys,

Brooklyn

The plane ride was eight hours. Riding first class never made me complain before. That was before I was waiting for hours to go back to the apartment I shared with my best friend, and he wasn't going to be there when I got back. Mariah didn't say a word the whole flight. She just looked out the window the whole time. I put my headphones on and just listened to music the entire time.

By the time we arrived back in the city, it was around 12:00 a.m. Waiting for us were Michael and Nick. They came to pick us up. I was expecting tears from Michael, but there were no wet eyes in sight. They seemed different, though. Not their usual selves. Nick didn't really say much. He gave me a hug and held on for a bit. Michael gave Mariah a slight hug, but he could tell she didn't really want one. The car ride back to campus was even quieter. Then Michael broke the silence, asking everyone about the holidays.

"Who cares about the holidays? What are we going to say to Brooklyn when we see her?" Mariah asks, her voice slightly cracking.

No one said anything. The car was quiet again. We didn't know what we were going to say to Brooklyn. We didn't know how she was doing.

When we all arrived back to campus late, we walked into Dylan and I's suite. There was Brooklyn sitting on the chair with someone there; I'm assuming it's her childhood friend, Elle. I hadn't ever met Elle, but she was pretty. She was like Brooklyn; they resembled each other strongly. Not even just their looks, but their body language. I noticed it immediately. You could tell Brooklyn was upset, but Elle was too. Elle was upset because Brooklyn was. That was a true friendship. They reminded me of Dylan and my friendship. What it felt like to have a platonic soulmate, a person who made you better and knew you better than anyone else.

Mariah called out Brooklyn's name, and she turned to see all four of us standing in the kitchen. She stood up immediately and walked toward us. She smiled slightly. Her eyes were puffy, and her brown eyes were watery. She came up to me first and held my hand in hers.

She looked at me and said, "I'm sorry, he was your best friend."

That's when I felt my tears come down. I was doing well with keeping my composure, but I couldn't hold it in after hearing that. I could feel the tears pouring quickly.

Brooklyn wiped my tears, and her eyes slightly started to water too. She just nodded and walked over to Mariah. She didn't say anything to her; she just looked at her. Mariah looked at us and brought us all into a hug, the three of us. For three years, it was always four of us in these hugs, and now it was down to three. The hug lasted for a while. Brooklyn and I cried; Mariah didn't. Which didn't surprise me because she never did.

After the hug broke apart, Brooklyn walked over to Nick and Michael. The two boys adored Dylan. He was the glue to their little trio. He was like their big brother, and they looked up to him. I think they thought they'd be able to be strong about it. They cried. They hugged Brooklyn too. It was something about Brooklyn. Everyone felt safe to be vulnerable around her. It was a vulnerable moment. What do you say when you lose someone you love?

Chapter Sixty-Three

Mariah Parker
Monday, December 5th, 2:15 a.m.

Brooklyn hadn't been back in the apartment. I know that for a fact. Everything was the way it was before. Her bed was untouched. She was at Dylan's the whole time. I got to meet Elle. She's amazing. I knew she would be. Brooklyn has told me about her, and I wished I had friends like that. I honestly hadn't kept in contact with any friends from my childhood. I was happy Elle was here with her. So, Brooklyn wasn't all alone. I wish I had been here, but mostly I felt so guilty. I kept replaying a conversation I had with Dylan on repeat. It was him asking me to protect Brooklyn if anything ever happened to him. I just thought, at the time, he was being dramatic. I didn't take it seriously enough. I had still made a promise that I would always keep her safe, and I was going to keep it. I always wondered what made Dylan tell me that. Did he know he would do something like this? Would he even do something like this? It didn't even seem like him. He loved Brooklyn too much.

Brooklyn did come back to the apartment with me. Her friend Elle came too and crashed in Brooklyn's bed. I figured she had been sleepy while staying up with Brooklyn for the past two nights. Brooklyn was just sitting on the couch again. Not saying a word and not moving at all.

"Hey," I said, as I sat beside her.

"Hi," she said, not looking away from the television. She was watching a cartoon; she hates cartoons.

"You're watching cartoons?" I asked.

"They were Dylan's favorite show," she answered.

I wanted to tell her about the promise I made to Dylan. Instead, I just kept it to myself. She looked at me, and I could see her eyes watering again. I looked down at my hands, so I wouldn't cry too.

The next morning, I had to leave early for an exam. It was a simple one for fashion merchandise. I finished in an hour. This week was essential; it was exam week. I was worried once Brooklyn told me she hadn't been to any of hers. I knew she was grieving, so I wondered if she was going to get to retake the ones she missed. I know school is the last thing on her mind now. I just worry. I don't think she'll ever be the same again. I walked back inside the apartment, and Brooklyn was sitting on the floor, just looking down. I looked at Elle, and she walked toward me.

"They're having his funeral on Wednesday," Elle said. "His mom sent the text to her this morning; she wants Brooklyn and all of his friends to speak at it."

A funeral? Already? I couldn't really think. I guess I just thought it was a dream everyone would wake up from.

I squatted down on the floor to talk to Brooklyn. She looked at me and didn't say anything. Suddenly, the news came on. I walked over to watch. I never liked the news. Recently, I learned how important the news is, especially in the city. The news released information about Elaine, Dylan's young step-grandma, who was found dead. They said that her cause of death was strangulation, and they're ruling it homicide. Lately, the police have been on high alert about almost everything. I looked back over at Brooklyn; I knew she had heard the news. She liked Elaine. Elaine was always nice; I had only met her once. She had gone to a game with Dylan's mom and sister one time. She was quiet, but she was always sweet. It's sad what happened to her. There's an open investigation, and there aren't any suspects so far. I guess Marcus would be one, but he was locked up way before she was murdered.

As the day went on, I was packing some of my things. After the funeral, I planned to leave to head back to Boston till the second semester. I had to pack up the bigger things to mail back to my house in Boston. I didn't have much room in my convertible. I was dreading leaving. I wasn't sure what Brooklyn's plan was. I didn't want her to just stay here alone. She was shutting everyone out, but I guess that's what people do when they grieve. I'm worried about her. Dylan meant the world to her; she adored him, and he adored her. It feels like everything is a part of some twisted nightmare that we're all going to wake up from and then laugh about it in the cafe. I didn't know what to expect at his funeral. Would they have his sister say something? What would everyone say? Would they play all his favorite songs? I've never been to a funeral. I never imagined what could happen after life. Would we be in heaven? Would we just stay asleep forever? I couldn't process it. I never lost anyone close to me before. I didn't want to imagine what life was like after death or if there was even an afterlife.

I was religious growing up. I went to church every Sunday. I listened to the gospel. I sang a few times with the choir. I feel like the older I got, the more I drifted away from God. I never wanted to. It just happened. It's my fault. I could have tried harder. I could have gone to church again; I could have prayed harder. It's just when everything was going wrong in my life, where was he? Why did it feel like he left me here to struggle? When I was harassed and abandoned, my family couldn't be more disappointed in me. Why? How was this "God's plan"? Now I have lost one of my closest friends. I could have helped Dylan more. I could have taken him more seriously. I could have gone to the authorities for him. I could have done more. I should have done more.

Chapter Sixty-Four

Brooklyn Reed
Wednesday, December 7th, 11:00 a.m.

I arrived at the church thirty minutes early. People were walking in the church and crowding around outside to talk. I couldn't. Not yet. I was sitting by the garden, looking at all the flowers. I noticed a white rose, my favorite flower. The flowers Dylan always got me. It hadn't sunk in yet that I had lost him. If I started to believe it, then it would come true. That's just the way things work. In my mind, I could hear Adele's "Make You Feel My Love" playing. It was a song that broke my heart every time it played. I was feeling black and blue. I was wearing my black dress. It was a bit too tight. The last time I wore this black dress was at a funeral years ago. My grandpa's funeral. People cried; I cried. People dropped to their knees and wept. I had to give a speech with my cousin that day. I saw significant others walking to pick up their loved ones after the viewing. I remember after the viewing, I had to walk outside because I couldn't believe my grandpa was just lying there. He was so still. The viewing. There wasn't a body. Dylan was never found. So what would be in his casket? Would it be his football uniform? His favorite blanket?

The thought of him being left in the water, unable to be found, made me sick.

I felt tears dripping down my dress from my eyes. I wiped my face, but more followed along. So many more. It felt bittersweet to be in a church. I love the church. I used to tell Dylan all these stories of me as a child running around in bible study, saying Easter speeches, and eating little mint candies during sermons. Dylan always wanted to become more religious. He told me his dad didn't believe in God. I wonder if his mom does. Dylan seemed pretty adamant about it. Once he put his mind to something, he meant it. I wish I got to spend more time loving him. I could have done it forever.

I noticed from a distance that Alicia was walking toward me, toward the garden. She looked pretty. Her hazel eyes were sparkling; I could tell she had been crying. She's wearing a black dress that looks expensive, paired with beautiful jewelry. She never wore designer things. She took a seat beside me.

"Hi, Brooke," she said with a smile.

I said, "Hey," back, keeping my face neutral.

"Today's going to be hard; I'm barely keeping it together," she said, her eyes beginning to water.

I take her hand and put it in mine. "It's going to be very hard, but I'm here if you need anything," I said, with tears coming down my face. She put her hand on my face and wiped my tears. Dylan used to do that.

"My boy loved you more than he ever loved anyone you know," she said.

I just looked at her, unable to form my words together.

"I look so silly today—all this fancy jewelry and outfit," she said with a laugh. "I'm only wearing this because Dylan liked it when I dressed up; he said it made me look so fancy."

"How am I supposed to go up there and tell them how much I loved him? I can barely hold it together now," I said.

"The most important thing to do is breathe," she said. We take a deep breath in and then breathe out together. "You know, Dylan, used to talk about you all the time. I remember the first day he ever mentioned you," she explained.

"When was that?" I asked.

"Freshman orientation," she answered.

"That was the day he and I met," I said.

"I remember. He called me and told me he was going to love you one day," she said, holding my hand.

"He knew that day?" I asked.

"He did," she answered.

"I wish I had more time with him," I said.

"Cherish the time you did have," she said with a kind nod. "You know, I was going through this box of his things. I found this beautiful necklace," she said, holding it up.

It's this beautiful rose gold necklace with my name on it. "He got this for me?" I asked.

"Yes. He was going to give it to you for Christmas. He wanted something real. So he used some savings he had," Alicia explained.

I hold the necklace in my hand, and I feel myself breaking down. She lost her son, and here I am making this about me. It wasn't fair. "I'm sorry; he was your son, and I should have done more," I rambled.

"You are allowed to grieve too, Brooklyn. He loved you. This is not your fault. I promise you that," she explained.

I nodded and hugged her.

"Never lose hope, Brooklyn. It's the most important thing a person should keep in their heart," she said quietly.

Chapter Sixty-Five

Dylan's Funeral: His Mother's Message

They say a mother's her son's first true love, and a son is a mother's last true love. As time has passed since I got the news about my son, that saying has been in my head. It was one of the first sayings I taught my son in Spanish. I wanted him to know that I loved him with every fiber of my being. He grew into such a strong and radiant young man. He overcame obstacles; I would have never been strong enough to. He made me proud every single day. Losing my firstborn has shown me how much I relied on him to keep me at peace. His phone calls every other day, with updates on his life, made my day. Seeing him fall in love with the most wonderful young woman is every mother's dream. Seeing him become a respectful gentleman showed me that my husband and I did a good job raising him. It felt weird waking up the first few days and not having a text from him. I keep wishing I could hear my son's voice one last time. I wish I could hear his laugh. I wish I could see him running around playing with Evie. I wish I could go back in time and cherish these moments more. My son is gone. My sweetest son. My first and only son. I miss you, Dylan. Today I can see the impact he had on everyone he met. I see how many of you are here to spread love and show support for Dylan and his loved ones.

No parent should have to bury their child. So if there are parents in here, hold your children so tightly because they are the most precious creation and they adore you so much. Dylan, my sweet son. I will miss you forever. Thank you for showing me how important it is to look for the light and joy in everything. I will be strong because you taught me to do so.

Chapter Sixty-Six

Dylan's Funeral: His Father's Message

My son knew I wasn't a man of many words, which I regret so much. I want to tell him how proud I am of him and everything he has accomplished in these short twenty-one years. His time on this earth was far too short. I would have given anything to go to another one of his games or just hear him tell me about things in his life. It wasn't until he got a bit older that I got to notice more about him, especially our similarities. He was the spitting image of me, my twin. It was funny the way our family was. Dylan and I were so similar, and Alicia and Evie were so similar. It made me realize how beautiful the creation of a family is. Something I wish I never took for granted. My son was my best friend. I wish I got to tell him that. He always knew how to make the hard days better and could lighten a room just with his smile. I would give anything to have more time with him. To see our family together once more. I'm sorry, Dylan. I didn't tell you enough how proud I was. I wasn't home as much as I should have been. I'm getting emotional; if only Dylan could see this. "What are the tears for, old man?" he'd say. Dylan, we will meet again someday. To my first born, I love you.

Chapter Sixty-Seven

Dylan's Funeral: His Sister's Message

Dylan was my big brother. I miss him so much. I wish we could play games again and watch movies. I love you.

Chapter Sixty-Eight

Dylan's Funeral: Reese's Message

Dylan Spencer. He's been like my brother since high school. He always stuck beside me, no matter what. No matter if it ruined his reputation or if he got pushed around because of it. Everyone knew not to mess with Dylan though. He was sweet; he was kind. But he knew when to put his foot down. I think the biggest thing I ever learned from Dylan was to never be afraid of putting your heart out there. He was an open book with Brooklyn. Always trying to be a better man than she would even think he would be. He gave it his all. One hundred percent of his all. I remember I used to sit back and admire it from afar. It was truly a blessing to be able to witness him fall in love and become the man we all knew he would be. Most importantly, he taught me to never be afraid. He said no matter, what he would protect me, whether I wanted him to or not, and he meant it. It never felt like he wouldn't be here. I thought he would always be here, and now that he's not, I don't know what to do.

My favorite memory with Dylan was one Halloween during our senior year. We went to this party. I knew he didn't want to go, but he went away. It was just us that night, and it was the first night I felt like I had a true friend. Dylan was my protector. He didn't play when it came to me. I miss him. I wish I could've had more time with him because time always went by so fast when it came to us. I'm happy I got to know him and experience the love he shared with everyone. I love you, Dylan.

Chapter Sixty-Nine

Dylan's Funeral: His Girlfriend's Message

When I first met Dylan, I knew I was going to fall in love with him. The feeling of comfort I got from him when I just met him was a feeling I never got with anyone else. He made me feel special. He made me feel safe. He made me feel warm. I had never had that feeling before. With Dylan, everything was easy. Falling in love with your partner in crime was the best blessing I ever had. I knew, at that moment, that God sent him to me. After all my cries to God, feeling hopeless and alone, he sent me someone to put me back together, piece by piece, which Dylan did. He allowed me to show him the worst sides of myself, and he still loved me as if it were the first time we ever met. He never lost that love for me; I could tell because I could see it all in his eyes.

I paused my speech. In the background of the church, I noticed a man walking in. He was an older, chubby man. He took a seat. I kept my eyes on him for a second, and he looked back at me. I continued with my speech.

Dylan was someone who made knowing him a true gift. His look of pure admiration whenever he says something to me is something I will never forget, and it's something I will miss the most. I had so much I wanted for us in this life, Dylan. You promised me you would never leave me, and I know you meant it when you said it. I love you forever, and not a day will go by where I don't miss your hands on my cheek. You were the purest person I ever met. My greatest love. You will have my heart forever.

Chapter Seventy

Dylan's Funeral: Mariah's Message

Goldilocks, you were the funniest person I knew. I loved our bickering and disagreements. Seeing how much you have changed everyone's world was the best thing I could have witnessed. No matter what, you always had your priorities in order, and you loved everything and everyone. I think the biggest thing you taught me was that it's okay to not be okay sometimes. You knew I was struggling with some things. You never said it. Or told me, but I know you knew. You always made sure I was okay, and for that, I'm so grateful. I have so much more I could say, but I'm afraid I can't do so without breaking down. So, Dylan, thank you. Thank you for giving me perspective and for letting me witness the gift, which was you. You were one of a kind, and I'm thankful I was able to be one of your friends.

On behalf of your football friends, Nick, Michael, and the rest of the team, they wanted to say that they loved you like a brother. These guys looked up to you and everything that you brought to the team and the brotherhood. Number three, may you rest in peace.

Chapter Seventy-One

Brooklyn Reed
Thursday, December 8th, 6:45 p.m.

J ust weeks ago, Elaine was here, and she was fine. Well, not fine, but alive. The police have nothing. Who would have done this to her? What motive did they have? I remember Dylan saying she was trying to warn him about people, but she never specified who she was talking about. It's not like I can go to the police; what information would I even have? I have no proof—no evidence of Elaine being trafficked. I just wondered why they haven't found her true identity yet. She's all over LAPD's radar, and her face is everywhere. They need to put together the pieces.

I had been cleaning out Dylan's suite. Reese went home the day of the funeral. Dylan's family wasn't really able to come in here and handle cleaning everything out, so I volunteered too. I figured it would be a good idea for me. I could get one last look around and see all his favorite things. I had already packed his bathroom and kitchen stuff in my car. I had just loaded his bedroom stuff into my car. I came back up to get the last of his things in the closet. It felt weird to see how empty the place was. All the decorations were taken down, and all the little messes were cleaned up. It was pretty much empty here. I was taping the box when I heard a knock at the door. I walked to the door, and I opened it. At the door was standing the man I saw at the funeral yesterday.

"Brooklyn?" he asked with a question.

"Yes," I answered.

"I'm Detective Clark. I met with Dylan on the day of his disappearance. We had a plan; we were going to get to the bottom of this. Next thing I knew, I saw his face on the news," the detective explained.

"I need you to explain everything to me," I demanded.

"The plan was for him to leave his car on the Brooklyn Bridge; he was supposed to meet me back at the diner. Hours went by, and he didn't show up. Then I saw the news," he explained.

"What was the goal of this plan?" I asked.

"Assassins are after him now, or they were. I know a lot about assassins, so I was trying to get him to hide until I found out who was behind this," he explained.

"How do you know so much about assassins? Aren't you a detective?" I asked.

"I was an assassin first, which is something I told Dylan that day," he answered.

"Dylan found out?" I asked.

"It wasn't hard for him to connect the dots. Once I was excused from the police academy for behavior, I went to Europe to clear my mind. Time went by, and I met these guys who were assassins, and they trained me," he explained.

"So you were killing people?" I asked.

"Yes, political figures, past convicts, anyone I was told to. But I stopped. Changed my name and came back to the United States under the name Hayden Clark," he said.

I crossed my arms. "Do you know anything about what happened to Dylan?" I asked.

"No, I don't know anything. His suicide was not the plan," he answered.

"So, you think it was suicide?" I asked.

"That's the only explanation for it, I believe. He seemed defeated and scared. It's not unlikely," he said.

Chapter Seventy-Two

Brooklyn Reed
Thursday, January 6th, 2:30 p.m.

The winter break almost flew by. But here in Florida, it wasn't really winter. I spent my time on the beach and hanging out with Elle. We shopped as much as we could. She still hasn't broken up with TJ, but I hope she does soon. They got into a disagreement while she and I went to dinner one night, so she spent the night upset. She went back to California yesterday; she's packing up her dorm, and she's transferring to Morrid. I was surprised she decided to do so too. She hates the cold, and LA was perfect for her. She just wasn't happy there, so she'll be moving in with Mariah and me for the spring semester. We got a three bedroom.

I walked down to the basement to get all my boxes to put in my car. Each semester, we needed to move out of the on-campus apartments completely, which is stupid. They do that for cleaning and maintenance. It's stupid, usually, but I won't be returning to the same apartment since I'll be in a three-bedroom apartment now. There was one box I specifically wanted to look through. It was the box of Dylan's things he left in my apartment. Inside were a few of his jackets and shirts. I took them all out to organize them. Under one of his hoodies was a piece of paper. It was wrinkled in a ball, like it had been ripped out of a notebook and thrown in or something. I unrolled the paper, and there was something written in black pen. It read, "I had to do it, baby. I had to keep you safe. I had to." That was all it said. It was in his handwriting. I felt my chest get unbearably heavy. When did Dylan write this? Why did Dylan write this?

Tethered to Hope

One and a Half Years Later

Acceptance. The final stage of grief. Accepting that a new reality can't be changed. What happened, happened. There's no running; there's no hiding. You see life differently. You appreciate life more. Even when a part of you is gone, you move on. Life goes on.

***

I received a call after not speaking for a year. I looked around my office with confusion.

"I never gave up looking for him, Brooklyn," says Lucas, rambling.

I wasn't sure where Lucas was going with this. I put my phone down for a second, and I picked it back up.

"What do you mean, Lucas?" I asked.

"I found something. Do you remember that phone I gave him? The one that was set to track and record everything?" Lucas explained.

"Yeah, I remember."

"Well, remember how he gave it back to me and took his actual phone back?"

"Yes," I say.

"That phone was never recovered from his SUV, was it?" Lucas asked.

"It wasn't," I answered. "Well, I put a tracker on that phone before I gave it back to him, and it has traveled from New York to Madrid, Spain. I think Dylan is alive, but he was kidnapped," explained Lucas.

I put my hand over my mouth to cover my shocked gasp. I wasn't sure if what I was hearing was true. I didn't want to get my hopes up for it to completely unravel and be untrue. A part of me never gave up either, and I wasn't going to. I accepted that he was gone. But what if he wasn't really gone? At least not in the way we thought he was. We never saw a body.

"How about we take a trip to Spain?" I asked.

About the Author

Maya Scott is a full-time student studying neuroscience. Her passion is to work in health care, assessing and researching Alzheimer's disease. Writing has been a passion of hers since she was a child. She started *Lingering Innocence* her senior year of high school and finished after a year of writing. While these are her two passions, she also has a passion for mental health. She strives to be a helping hand for those who need it, a shoulder to cry on, and someone people can go to if they just need someone to listen.

Resources

National Sexual Assault Hotline: 1-800-656-4673
Suicide and Crisis Lifeline: 988
TheHopeLine: www.thehopeline.com

Milton Keynes UK
Ingram Content Group UK Ltd.
UKHW041003040324
438885UK00006B/452